Deadly Consequences
Based on a True Story

R. M. Russell

Just Chilling Press—Granbury, TX
ISBN: 979-8-9871374-0-6
eBook ISBN: 979-8-9871374-1-3
Library of Congress Control Number: 2022920376
Title: *Deadly Consequences*
Author: R. M. Russell
Digital distribution | 2022
Paperback | 2022

This is a work of fiction based on a true story. The characters, names, incidents, places, and dialogue are products of the author's imagination, and are not to be construed as real.

Dedication

This book is dedicated to my son; he was my strength and inspiration when writing this book. I love you with all my heart.

A big thank you to all the family, friends, and people who had never even met him who heard this story and stood by him during this tragic ordeal.

Table of Contents

Preface

The story will lead you through the horrific side of the world of online adult advertising and how dangerous just one encounter can be. Your life will never be normal again. This organized crime group has perfected their skills to lure in unsuspecting men and women responding to an advertisement for a massage and then to commit crimes against them. The people in this group are well-trained in weapons and tactics and how to deploy against their victims. You will read about organized crime and how the law protects them at the highest levels. We will show you the dark side of what happens when you reach out online and the carnage that follows. You can follow the evidence and discover for yourself where police officers and detectives failed their duty time and time again. Continue to walk the path of the investigation with every turn of the page. I must admit I am personally connected to this case, but I will attempt to remain objective. You will have insight into information, you will be given details and know what the evidence was or wasn't, and you will be able to make a truly objective decision. Most of you have played a detective game like "Clue." Was it Mrs. White in the library with a candlestick? Well, imagine that everyone gathers at the table to play the game and the cards are passed out. Player 1 (The District Attorney) immediately yells out "I know the answer, it was Professor Plum in the study with a knife," and declares himself the winner, game over! We all know he is wrong, and everyone says, "Player 1, you're wrong, and we can prove it," but Player 1 states, "It's my game, it was Professor Plum, and that's it. I am the winner." Folks, that basically describes how a lot of cases are closed in the criminal courts today. Prosecutors stand before the courts and jurors and lie and mislead them every day. Is it fair? No. "Innocent until prover guilty"? No. But if you or a family member or friend find yourself on the wrong side of the law, innocent or guilty, you will unfortunately understand the cold, hard truth about justice in today's legal system. Lady Liberty has left the building. You are going to hear the truth here, from beginning to the end, then you will see the jury's verdict, and this gripping true story will come to its astonishing "conclusion." Then, you can decide if justice was served.

In our legal system we have the chance to be judged by a jury of our peers, and it has been the best system on earth, but can we still say that? Don't be confused. The judge oversees the courtroom, and the prosecutors are supposed to seek truth and justice through a methodical process of following evidence no matter where it leads; but the 12 jurors who sit in judgement over a defendant are in effect the judge, jury, and executioner. When they decide guilt or innocence, in most cases that is final. Yes, there are appeals; but only about 1% percent of verdicts are overturned on appeal. Very few are even reviewed at all. Are there innocent men and women in our prison system today? Yes, there are, and far more than anyone of us can truly know about. Today, everyone is polarized on one side or another. It is almost impossible for two people to agree on anything. Can anyone get a fair trial by their peers in this social climate? Can we legitimately get a fair verdict of guilt or innocence from 12 men and women? With daily prosecutorial misconduct in the courtroom, can anyone expect a fair and unbiased trial? As you go through this true story of the events on that evening in November 2017 and the events that followed, you may begin asking the same questions that I have proposed to you.

Cast of Characters

Organized Crime Players

Cashman – This guy has been running illegal activities for decades. He had a 2010 conviction for money laundering and aiding and abetting. In June 2022, he was arrested by the FBI and charged with similar crimes, but the District Attorney prosecuting this case insists he is not involved. (This is a critical piece of evidence to consider as you continue through this true crime novel.)

Jade – A one-time victim of Cashman, but with a twist. Jade willingly turned to performing organized criminal activity, moving from prey to predator. She is referenced as the "bottom girl." This title is usually for the second in charge of the operation who is responsible for all the other team members.

Cinnamon – From broken home, runaway, drug addict, prostitute, she turned to violent crimes such as theft, robbery, kidnapping, and trafficking

Sapphire – Similar story as Cinnamon, was recruited by Jade from the Texas Panhandle with the promise of making it big with lots of money. She turned to a life of crime, drugs, theft, robbery, kidnapping, terroristic threats, and more.

Yet to be identified – 4th Team Member at the scene – Never formally identified. The law enforcement agencies never investigated this person and never attempted to locate them. All we know is that they arrived at the scene with Jade, Cinnamon, and Sapphire. Could it have been Cashman? He was at the scene that night.

Junior – Son of Cashman. Runs operations in the Houston area. He was arrested and convicted of murder in 2022. He had a team member at a victim's apartment. His team member called him and stated that the mark (victim) was not cooperating. He called a friend, and they went together to the apartment. He told his team member to wait downstairs. A couple of minutes later, they executed the victim. Keep in mind as we continue, this is a very dangerous and violent organized crime group that has perfected their crimes.

Nikki – Cashman's daughter. Seems to work behind the scenes but was a main contact on the night in question. Sapphire kept texting her, asking her what she should do. Nikki told her to clean up the scene and do not talk to law enforcement, tell them nothing!

The Police Major Players

Sgt. Smith – After 4 days into the prosecution's case, Sgt. Smith reluctantly stated that she was the lead detective in charge. Her title with the police department lists her as department services, not detective. Sgt. Smith was the last law enforcement witness for the state; and by this time, all other law enforcement officers had clearly stated they were not in charge of the investigation and did not know who was. A homicide investigation where no-one knew who the lead detective was to report to? She had zero experience working a homicide case.

Texas Ranger – He had 20 plus years of experience, top cop on the scene with more experience and training than any other officer or Detective in the county, but not the lead detective and stated that he was not in charge and he did not know who was in charge. Cover up? Lies? How did the Texas Ranger not know who was in charge? He was the top cop in the county and had statewide jurisdiction. He was the only one to interview Sapphire, and he was also the only one to interview Michael. He oversaw submitting evidence to the state crime lab but was not in charge of the investigation. This begs the question of why no-one wanted to take charge of this investigation.

Crime Scene Investigator – **Ms. Mann** – This was a civilian, not certified in Crime Scene Evidence (CSI). She took evidence to her home the night of the crime and did not maintain a chain of custody for any evidence collected, and she was not in charge of the evidence that she collected.

911 Caller – Mr. Martz – He was just on his way to a concert with his wife that evening.

First officer on Scene – **Officer Walters** – Not experienced in crime scene preservation, he touched and shook the women. disturbing evidence and kept running back and forth between the two women, contaminating the crime scene. He had no clue of what to do.

Medical Examiner – Testified that the two women were shot and died instantly at the scene.

Fire Department Employee/Phone Finder – Was working a motor vehicle accident on the interstate when he picked up a phone out of a puddle of water in the ditch on the side of the highway.

DPS Crime Lab – Testified that Michael's DNA was excluded from the phone found on the side of the highway, meaning Michael had not been in contact with it.

The Defense

Previous Victim – Another victim of the crime organization who came forward to testify about how dangerous this organization is.

Mom – What can you say, a mom's love shines bright during testimony.

Daughter – Terrified as you might expect being on the witness stand but firmly standing by her father.

Ex-Wife – Although married to Michael at the time of the incident, this relationship was always doomed to fail. Michael loved his wife and tried his best to give her everything she needed and wanted, but nothing was ever good enough to keep her faithful.

Use of Force Expert – Gave testimony on how, why, and when self-defense should be appropriate to use.

Forensics Ballistics Expert – Gave testimony on the crime scene and how he can tell the movements and positioning of Cinnamon and Jade before and after they were shot.

FBI/Trafficking Expert – Testified about sex trafficking and when victims turn to predators.

Michael – Testified on his own behalf and gave a full and powerful accounting of the day before and the day of the incident.

Chapter 1
The Organized Crime Boss

In March 2010, Cashman pleaded guilty to money laundering and aiding and abetting and was sentenced by a federal court judge to 60 months in federal prison and ordered to pay a $20,000 fine. He was remanded into custody following that sentencing hearing.

According to documents filed from May 2004 to approximately August 1, 2008, Cashman was part of an interstate prostitution ring advertising their business on the Internet under the guise of an escort service. Women provided the prostitution services, traveling from Texas to numerous cities including Chicago, New York City and Boston, to engage in prostitution with men solicited through Internet advertising.

"The defendants in this case laundered their ill-gotten profits in order to fuel the continuation of their illicit Internet-based prostitution enterprise," according to a Special Agent in Charge of the IRS Criminal Investigation Division Field Office. "These sentences should serve as a deterrent to those who might contemplate similar criminal conduct."

The prostitutes were paid for their services by credit cards and cash deposited into an account controlled by Cashman at Bank of America. The proceeds from the accounts were used to promote and perpetuate the interstate prostitution enterprise by purchasing airline tickets, hotel accommodations, and paying advertising expenses. The prostitution proceeds were also used to make a down-payment on a luxury automobile and to make payments on a home. Both a Bentley and the home were used by Cashman as a backdrop for photos used on Internet ads that promoted their prostitution services.

"The financial transactions noted above were financial transactions involving financial institutions and affected interstate and foreign commerce. The transactions were made with what Cashman knew to be proceeds from interstate prostitution and transactions were conducted for the purpose of promoting and carrying on the interstate enterprise."

Did this sentence deter Cashman from similar conduct? No, it did not. Instead, he expanded his interstate and international organized crime syndicate to include robbery, forceful entry, kidnapping, terroristic threats, aggravated assault, threats using a deadly weapon, trafficking, and murder.

Cashman was arrested and charged with similar charges as above in November 2021 and has since accepted another plea deal with federal prosecutors in June 2022. At the time of the writing of this book, he is still awaiting formal sentencing by a federal judge.

Does anyone think this little bump in the road and another couple of years in a federal penitentiary and a couple of years of probation will even slow down this organized crime syndicate? The government will take what property and funds they can locate, slap him on the wrist for all the lives he has ruined and all the destruction and carnage he has caused, and pat themselves on the back for what they consider to be a job well done.

Chapter 2
The First Encounter

Michael was surfing the internet one day and came upon a site for an erotic massage. He went for a regular massage a few times a month anyway so, he made contact and soon after made an appointment for a massage. He wanted to be safe, this was his first time for an erotic massage, and he did not know what to expect, so he thought it would be safer to set the appointment at his place of business. The online organization agreed to the location and, that eased his anxiety level a bit. He felt everything would be okay.

"It's at my job, lots of people around and we have police on-site if there is a problem."

Michael was a nurse working in an administrative position at a large hospital, so there were always a lot of people and security around. Well, the appointment day came. It was on a Friday afternoon. He went out to meet the massage therapist; and to his surprise, there were two of them.

They were young and attractive, and he thought, "Okay, two for the price of one."

He walked with the women into the building past security check-in and into his office. Everything seemed normal at this point, so he was feeling pretty good about his decision, even though he hired the massage therapist on the internet. Cinnamon told him to get undressed for the massage, so Michael complied and stripped down to his boxers.

So, there he was, stripped down to his boxers, ready for a massage, and he jokingly said, "Hey, it would be nice if you both undressed as well."

Then, Cinnamon told him to sit down in a chair; and Sapphire leaned over and stated, "Oh, you didn't think we were prostitutes, did you?"

Shocked and confused at what she said, he replied "Of course I didn't think you were prostitutes. I really did not know what to expect from an erotic massage, but we are at my place of business, and I want to keep things professional."

Then they told him they wanted $5,000 each or they would start screaming rape. Michael was stripped down to his boxers, sitting in a chair, and now the two women are demanding a large sum of money. The two women began digging through his office. At this point, he was scared and confused at what was happening, with all kinds of things flashing through his mind and none of them good.

They began threatening him, "We will yell rape."

"We will call the police."

They picked up a picture of Michael and his family and stated, "That is a pretty little girl in the picture. Is that your daughter?"

Michael replied, "Yes."

Then Cinnamon said, "If you don't give us the money, we will traffic her. You know, guys just love little girls."

At this point, he just wanted them to leave. He told them he did not have that much cash. Cinnamon threw his clothes at him and said, "Get dressed."

He complied and got dressed as fast as he could.

Cinnamon then said, "You're coming with us, and we're going to your bank."

That's when they showed him a gun that they had in a large leather bag that Cinnamon carried on her shoulder. There were patients and other employees in the building, and Michael did not want anyone to get hurt. He knew the situation could get even worse in a hurry since they had a gun. They took him to their vehicle and told him to get in the back seat.

Then Cinnamon asked, "Where do you bank, asshole?"

"Chase," Michael replied.

They started driving to his bank. The child safety locks were activated on the car door, and he couldn't get out of the back door himself. He was trapped. At the bank, Sapphire opened the back door and told Michael to get out. Cinnamon showed him the gun again and told him to walk in front of her. They walked him into the bank, Sapphire beside him and Cinnamon directly behind him. Cinnamon told him he had better not mess this up and that if he did anything it would be his last mistake. Michael withdrew all the money in his account, about $8,000 and turned it over to Sapphire when they returned to the vehicle.

Cinnamon stated, "That's only $8,000. We need more money, and we will get it from you or your daughter, it does not really matter to us."

Cinnamon and Sapphire had noticed another bank card in his wallet when they rifled through it, and they proceeded to drive to the second bank. At this point, Michael was terrified, wondering if he would ever see his family again or would these two women kill him. If he could not get them enough money, were they going to go after his daughter? Was someone already going after his family?

Michael just knew, "This is it. I am going to die."

Again, they got him out of the back seat and walked him into the bank. This time there was no money in the account.

Back in the car, they asked, "Where is your money, asshole?"

They were very upset and again began threatening him and his family. Trembling, Michael, said "You have all my money there is no more, I can't give you what I don't have."

They drove around a little while, and then they stopped the vehicle in a secluded and shady side of town. Michael thought "Oh, shit this is it, I am going to die. Will my family even find my body? Will these women traffic my daughter as they have threatened? Oh, God help me!"

At this point, Sapphire got out of the vehicle, opened the car door, and said, "Get the fuck out."

Then she got back in the car, and they sped off. So, there he was, standing in the middle of the street, trying to figure out where he was; but at least he was alive, so he began walking until he figured out where he was and then walked back to work. At this point, he was just happy to be alive, and the nightmare seemed to be over. He called his wife to make sure everything was okay, nothing going on out of the ordinary, no strange calls or vehicles outside, nothing. Why didn't he call the police? These women had told him that if he called the police they would know because they have police working for them. He had no reason not to believe them when they told him that. Cinnamon told him that they would traffic his daughter and kill his family if he called the police. So, he went home and did not call the police and did not tell anyone, just thanking God that the nightmare was over and he was alive and his family was safe.

Chapter 3
The Second Encounter

On a Saturday morning in November in north Texas, there was a slight breeze and the sun was shining bright. It was about 60 degrees. No better time than a Texas morning in the Fall. Michael took his wife and daughter to eat breakfast that morning, then went to get a haircut as his wife and daughter went to get their nails done. At this time, his family was living with his parents as Michael and his wife had just sold their home and were in the process of building another home nearby. After spending the morning with his wife and daughter, he returned home and then went jogging with his little brother, which he frequently did on weekends. After the Friday encounter with Cinnamon and Sapphire, Saturday was even more beautiful than usual; and everything seemed to be going great. He could not have asked for a better day. When Michael and his little brother got home, they both took showers to get all the pollens off of them, changed clothes, and then went to his little brother's room to play video games. Then, late that afternoon, he started getting text messages from an unknown number. He tried to ignore them, but they just kept coming. Then he received a call, and it was Cinnamon.

She said they were on the way to his house. He quickly got up and left the room and told them, "Do not come to my house."

They replied, "Then meet us somewhere."

He asked where, and they said, "Just get in your car and drive, and we will tell you where to stop."

Michael was scared. "Could this really be happening again?"

Worried about his family, he decided to do as they ordered him to do. He went downstairs, went to his safe in the garage where he had $2,100 in cash, and took it out in hopes it would be enough to make them leave him alone. On his way out the door, his dad told him dinner was almost ready.

Michael said, "Okay, I will be right back. I'm just going out for a few minutes. I will be back for dinner."

Michael got into his vehicle and began driving. After about 10 minutes, he began to get text messages from someone from the crime organization. He was not sure who it was because the number they called from came in as "unknown," but he knew it was them.

They asked, "What are you close to right now?"

Michael told them he was coming up on a church.

They texted him, "Do not stop there. What is coming up next?"

Michael replied, "A bank just ahead."

The person told him, "Pull into the bank, send us the address, and wait for us."

Michael was terrified, with all kinds of thoughts racing through his mind at this point. "Why are they wanting to meet me? Are they coming back to make sure there are no witnesses? Why are they wanting to meet me again? Oh, God, help and protect me, I am so terrified I can't even think straight. It's Saturday evening (about 6:30 pm), and all the banks are closed, and they know they cleared out my bank account yesterday."

He kept moving, driving around the bank parking lot from front to back so hopefully he would not be a sitting target. After about 20-30 minutes, two cars aggressively pulled into the bank parking lot and parked on the east side of the bank.

Michael pulled up behind their vehicles and held out an envelope containing the $2,100 and said, "This is it, this is all I have left. Please take it and leave me and my family alone."

Then, a woman that he had never met before, Jade, stated, "Is this a joke? Do you think we are playing a game here, you fucking asshole?"

Michael replied, "No, I do not think this is a game, I know you're serious."

Then Cinnamon jumped into Michael's vehicle and sat right behind him in the rear seat. (Michael drove a Hyundai, and when you put the vehicle in park the doors automatically unlock). Jade went around and got into the front passenger seat. Jade ordered Michael to pull into a parking space just to the left side of her vehicle. Michael told the two women to get out of his vehicle, but Jade told him that was not going to happen, that was not how this was going to play out. Cinnamon still had that oversized leather bag from the day before, you know, the one with the gun in it. The two women, Cinnamon and Jade, began digging through his car, digging in the center console and glove box. Jade ordered Michael to give her his wallet, and that is exactly what he did. Michael knew he was outnumbered. He had seen two vehicles pull in with two people in each vehicle, so there were two people with Michael in his vehicle and two people outside somewhere. Jade took the keys out of the ignition and then took his cell phone. She then made a phone call and began to read out the information on his credit card to someone on the line. The women were very aggressive and knew exactly what they were doing, taking tactical positioning both inside and outside the vehicle and demanding money, money he did not have. They told Michael they had someone 10 minutes from his parents' home and that if he did not do what they said they would make a call and everyone would be killed and his 14-year-old daughter trafficked.

Jade threw his wallet at him and said, "Get the fuck out of the car. Now! You are coming with us."

It was November, around 6:40 pm. The sun had begun to go down. He had no more money with him and no way to get any more money. Michael could only think about his family back home who had no idea what was happening or what might be headed their way. It was late on a Saturday night. Cinnamon opened the door and tugged at Michael's arm to get him out of the car. His wallet was laying in the floorboard after Jade threw it at him; and as he bent down to get his wallet out of the floorboard, in the corner of his eye he saw his handgun under the seat. He had forgotten it was even there. Between selling his home, being in the process of building another home, and moving in with his parents, he had things in storage, in his parents' garage, and in his cars.

At this point he heard Cinnamon say, "Get in my car right fucking now. If you fuck with us, you're dead."

Michael pulled his gun from underneath his seat and loaded the chamber and said, "I am not getting into that car again. I am not going anywhere with you."

Furious, Cinnamon stated, "That's the last fucking mistake you're ever going to make" and began reaching into that bag that she had a gun in the day before.

Michael was terrified. He fired one time. That shot struck Cinnamon in the side of her head, killing her instantly. He then turned and told Jade to give him his keys and phone and just leave, just please leave him alone and leave. But remember, Jade had told him that was not how this game would play out. These aggressive, well-trained women would not do that. Jade started moving towards him, reaching for his gun. Michael fired one more shot, striking Jade in an upwards direction in the neck. The bullet exited through her head, killing her instantly. Meanwhile, Sapphire had stayed in the other vehicle and never got out, so she and never posed a direct threat to him at the time. She moved to the driver 's position in the vehicle and drove away, so Michael never pursued her and never fired at her. Although he was within very close range to Sapphire, she did not pose an immediate threat to him. He could easily have fired a third round and shot Sapphire, and Sapphire acknowledged this fact later in court, but he did not do that because she did not attack him at that moment, even though she had robbed him and kidnapped him the day before. To this day, Michael does not know where the fourth person went or who they were. The police investigators never tried to identify the fourth person.

Michael was in shock, as you can imagine. He was scared. He had just killed two people and was afraid that someone was already on the way to his parents' house to kill everyone. He picked up his keys and phone off the ground where Jade had dropped them and got into his car and started for home. When Michael was backing up his vehicle, he accidently backed up over Cinnamon, not even realizing it at the time. All he could think about at the time was that someone was on their way to kill his family. He drove straight home and sat outside for a little while, waiting to see if anyone showed up. After a while, it looked like no-one was coming. Still in shock and not thinking straight, he knew that he did not want that gun anymore, so he took it and put it in a field in a pile of brush. Then he went and got gas and went through an automatic car wash. He didn't even really know why. Then he went back to the house and walked in, carefully scanning the room. He went through the dining room, into the kitchen. His mom and dad were sitting on the couch in the living room, and his little brother was on the loveseat. His wife and daughter were upstairs. His dad told him that his dinner was in the fridge, but he replied that he was not hungry. Everything seemed to be okay, so he went upstairs. His wife was in the shower, and his daughter was in her bedroom. Again, all seemed to be okay. He waited for his wife to get out of the shower, then he went in and showered. For now, no one had come to the house for his family.

He could not sleep at all that night, he just laid there next to his wife, silent, with the events of the evening replaying in his head over and over. He knew he had to turn himself in to the police first thing in the morning. It seemed so surreal and dreamlike.

"Did that just happen? Did I just kill two people? I am going first thing in the morning and turn myself in while everyone is at church. Yes, that is what I am going to do."

Chapter 4
The Crime Scene

It was a nice fall evening. There is nothing quite like Texas in the Fall. The temperatures in the afternoons and evenings are usually high 60's to mid-70 degrees with just a slight breeze. This beautiful November evening was stained by organized crime and the criminal carnage that follows in its wake. You already know the defendant had to use self-defense to keep from being kidnapped a second time and to save his own life and the life of his family. On this evening, at a bank located off the highway lay the bodies of Jade and Cinnamon, the two women who had called Michael and ordered him to meet them somewhere. Were they shot and killed because they were robbing, threatening bodily harm to Michael and his family, and attempting to kidnap Michael, not to mention being in his vehicle against his will, which in Texas is the same thing as breaking and entering your home, or did the defendant lose control?

Let's look at the crime scene. Jade body was located between Michael's vehicle and her vehicle, and she was lying at the rear of the vehicle. According to Michael, Jade was moving towards him and reaching for his weapon. If Michael was at the back of his vehicle by the trunk and Jade body fell forward, then that supports Michael's side of the events. What about Cinnamon?

She was about 4-6 feet behind Michael's vehicle. We know when she was ordering Michael get in her vehicle, she was facing him; but the bullet entered on the side of her head.

Michael stated that Cinnamon said, "That will be the last fucking mistake you make." And began to reach into her bag. If you reach across your body and are twisting to get into a bag that is on your opposite shoulder, your head and body will twist. Again, Michael's description of the events is proven by ballistic experts.

Let's look at the scene from above. We have two bodies lying on the ground, both with gunshot wounds to the head, both deceased and lying in their own pool of blood. There is also the third woman, Sapphire. She had pulled across the street until Michael left and then returned to the scene. Did she call 911? No, she did not. She called Cashman and his daughter, Nikki, and they told her not to talk to police but to clean up the crime scene. The fourth person is a mystery because the investigators for some reason did not attempt to find him/her.

Mr. Martz entered the scene, stopping at the ATM on his way to town for a concert when he came across the scene. He stated that when he pulled up, he noticed Sapphire taking things off the bodies and one item in particular appeared to be a phone. He stated that the left driver door of the vehicle that Jade was driving was open. Both of these last details will be important as we keep going through the story. In just few minutes the first officer on the scene, Officer

Walters, has arrived. He seemed unsure of what to do, running between the bodies while he waited for backup to arrive.

Chapter 5
The Texas Ranger

The history of the Texas Rangers spans nearly 200 years. Thousands of Rangers patrolled the frontier, fought in military battles, and arrested cattle rustlers. Their story contains heroic acts of bravery but also some moments that challenge our idea of the Rangers as noble lawmen. They protected settlers and enforced laws but also sometimes executed thieves without a trial, drove Native American tribes from their homelands, and some Rangers even lynched Mexicans and Mexican-Americans along the Texas-Mexico border. Modern Texas Rangers, like FBI agents, are highly trained investigators who assist local authorities on everything from homicides to public corruption cases. They must be versatile, especially in rural areas, where they may be called on to do just about anything.

Now let's look at the Texas Ranger in this case. He was called to the scene at a bank off of the highway and was told there were two deceased females. When he arrived, he looked over the scene and then met with the officers already at the scene and Ms. Mann, an unlicensed and uncertified civilian serving as the crime scene investigator. He began by getting updated information from the officers on scene and was told that a witness, Sapphire, was in the back of a patrol vehicle but that what little she was saying was not believable. He went and took Sapphire out of the patrol vehicle and walked her over to his vehicle to interview her. You will find the rest of the interview in a later chapter, and what you will read will shock you to your core, as she continues to lie and give false statements throughout the interview and never tells the Ranger the whole story or the truth. What you thought you knew about the justice system, innocent until proven guilty and following the evidence wherever it may lead you to the truth is only pretty words that no longer apply in our current justice system today.

After interviewing Sapphire, the Ranger meet Michael at the county jail, where he interviewed him for about 20 minutes. I know you must be asking yourself, "This is a homicide investigation, there are two deceased bodies, and he only interviewed the suspect for only approximately 20 minutes?" At this point after interviewing Sapphire, the Ranger had a good idea that there was more to this story, so why only question Michael for 20 minutes? Did the Ranger even want the truth, or was the Ranger told not to press Michael for his side of the events? Keep in mind that Modern Texas Rangers, like FBI agents, are highly trained investigators; so why stop after such a short interview?

Chapter 6
The Eyewitness Interview

INTERVIEW OF Sapphire, on the night of the incident.

TEXAS RANGER: I'm at the bank, about to conduct a witness interview related to a double homicide that happened earlier this evening. How old are you, sweetie?

SAPPHIRE: I'm 23.

TEXAS RANGER: Okay. Not every night something like this happens; huh?

SAPPHIRE: No. I never really been involved in something like this.

TEXAS RANGER: Are you scared?

SAPPHIRE: Yeah, I'm really terrified.

TEXAS RANGER: Okay. I understand that. What's your name

SAPPHIRE: Sapphire.

TEXAS RANGER: Do you know your driver's license number?

SAPPHIRE: No.

TEXAS RANGER: Do you have any ID with you?

SAPPHIRE: Un-uh.

TEXAS RANGER: So, you've never had a license before just recently?

SAPPHIRE: No, sir.

TEXAS RANGER: Really?

SAPPHIRE: Yeah. I mean, no, I have not.

TEXAS RANGER: Being 23?

SAPPHIRE: I know.

TEXAS RANGER: No license before?

SAPPHIRE: No.

TEXAS RANGER: Are you from around here?

SAPPHIRE: No, I'm from the Panhandle.

TEXAS RANGER: Panhandle girl, huh?

SAPPHIRE: Yeah.

TEXAS RANGER: All right. Here's the thing before we even get started. I understand—how many people have asked you questions so far?

SAPPHIRE: Four or five.

TEXAS RANGER: Four or five? I'm probably going to ask you some of the same things that have already been asked. Okay?

SAPPHIRE: Yeah.

TEXAS RANGER: What I want you to do is, and I don't know all these people out here. I know most of them, but I don't know all of them. Okay, so if anybody out here scared the shit out of you and made you think that you were about to go to jail and all that other stuff, I'm here to tell you the only thing that you can get in trouble for from this point forward is if we find out that you're lying about anything. Okay?

SAPPHIRE: Oh, okay.

TEXAS RANGER: Because this is a homicide investigation. Okay?

SAPPHIRE: Yeah, I know. I'm not lying about anything.

TEXAS RANGER: And lying in a homicide investigation is a crime.

SAPPHIRE: Will get you in a lot of trouble.

TEXAS RANGER:—This is a pretty serious matter.

SAPPHIRE: Yeah.

TEXAS RANGER: Okay. But I'm here to tell you, otherwise, I'm not interested in jamming you up on anything, and we'll get more into all that later, but like I said, I don't know what all has been told to you, what hasn't, so I wanted to rest your mind that I'm not sitting here with any interest in all in seeing you go to jail. That's not what my interest is. Okay?

SAPPHIRE: Yeah.

TEXAS RANGER: All right. I've been told that you were riding in that vehicle that's parked right there.

SAPPHIRE: In the Honda?

TEXAS RANGER: Right. Is that right?

SAPPHIRE: Yeah, I was in the passenger seat. I wasn't driving it. We were going to go get something to eat, and they were like, "We've got to meet somebody really quick." And I was like, "Okay." You know. I didn't think anything of it. I don't know who this person is. I don't know who they were meeting. So, we go and we pull up at the bank and he pulls up as well. And they got in his car; and not even five minutes later, they were both out; and he shot her and then shot her.

TEXAS RANGER: Okay. All right. Well, let's back up a little bit and let's kind of get into the weeds a little bit of what happened. Who was the girl that you were riding with, what's her name?

SAPPHIRE: Cinnamon.

TEXAS RANGER: How old is Cinnamon? Do you know?

SAPPHIRE: She's 21.

TEXAS RANGER: Twenty-one. Okay. Where did she live?

SAPPHIRE: She lived with me. She lives with me. We all live together. We're all roommates.

TEXAS RANGER: Okay. All right. The girl that's driving Honda… Is that Cinnamon's car?

SAPPHIRE: No, they're both Jade's boyfriend's cars, but he just bought it for us.

TEXAS RANGER: Who's Jade's boyfriend?

SAPPHIRE: Cashman.

TEXAS RANGER: Cashman.

SAPPHIRE: Cashman. That's not his name.

TEXAS RANGER: That's his street name, right?

SAPPHIRE: But—yeah.

TEXAS RANGER: Cashman. Okay. And how old is Cashman?

SAPPHIRE: I don't know.

TEXAS RANGER: What color is Cashman?

SAPPHIRE: Black.

TEXAS RANGER: Okay. Do you know where he lives?

SAPPHIRE: He lives with Jade. He lives with us.

TEXAS RANGER: He lives there with you all?

SAPPHIRE: Yeah.

TEXAS RANGER: Okay. And I'm going to assume that Jade is the girl that was driving the Mercedes; is that right?

SAPPHIRE: Yes, sir.

TEXAS RANGER: How old is Jade?

SAPPHIRE: She's 23.

TEXAS RANGER: Okay. Have you called Cashman and let him know about it?

SAPPHIRE: Yeah, he was asking if everything was okay and stuff and what the address was and everything. That's about it.

TEXAS RANGER: Okay. Who else have you called?

SAPPHIRE: That's it.

TEXAS RANGER: That's it?

SAPPHIRE: Yeah.

TEXAS RANGER: Okay. I'll probably want to talk to him, too. How long have you all lived together over there?

SAPPHIRE: I'd say about six, seven months. I've known him for a while though.

TEXAS RANGER: How did you meet him?

SAPPHIRE: Through Facebook but I've known him for a while.

TEXAS RANGER: Okay. All right. And where do you work?

SAPPHIRE: I don't work.

TEXAS RANGER: Don't work? Okay. Where does Cinnamon, did Cinnamon work?

SAPPHIRE: No, they don't work right now.

TEXAS RANGER: Okay. And where does Cashman work?

SAPPHIRE: I don't know. I don't really pay attention to all of that.

TEXAS RANGER: Okay. Is Cashman unemployed

SAPPHIRE: He owns his own business. I know, like that's all I know. I really don't ask him his business.

TEXAS RANGER: Has he lived there the whole time?

SAPPHIRE: Well, yeah. They're together.

TEXAS RANGER: Okay. Him and Jade?

MS Sapphire: Yeah.

TEXAS RANGER: Okay. But you live there with him six or seven months and you don't know what his business is.

SAPPHIRE: We live in separate rooms and stuff like that.

TEXAS RANGER: So, you really don't know much.

SAPPHIRE: I don't talk to him very much. I mean, we'll talk but, I mean, they're together (Cashman and Jade.) Why would I talk to him? That's all I know.

TEXAS RANGER: For six, seven months. Okay. do you have a boyfriend or anything?

SAPPHIRE: No, sir. I'm single.

TEXAS RANGER: Single? Never been married. not divorced or anything?

SAPPHIRE: Nah.

TEXAS RANGER: You got any kids?

SAPPHIRE: Yeah, I have twins.

TEXAS RANGER: Do they live there with you?

SAPPHIRE: No. They live with the father. I don't have any custody of my kids.

TEXAS RANGER: Okay. Why is that, if you don't mind me asking?

SAPPHIRE: I really don't know. Honestly, the baby daddy just doesn't like me. That's all I have to say.

TEXAS RANGER: Okay. Have you been in jail before for anything?

SAPPHIRE: Yeah, only for like traffic problems. That's it. Like no license and stuff.

TEXAS RANGER: Okay. what about the other two girls? Have they been in any trouble that you know of?

SAPPHIRE: No, I don't know. Honestly, I don't.

TEXAS RANGER: They haven't? What about Cashman?

SAPPHIRE: No.

TEXAS RANGER: No?

SAPPHIRE: No trouble at all. Nothing.

TEXAS RANGER: So, what time did you get up today?

SAPPHIRE: I got up around noonish.

TEXAS RANGER: Okay. Who all was at the house when you got up?

SAPPHIRE: Just me, Jade, and Cinnamon.

TEXAS RANGER: Okay.

SAPPHIRE: We just got up, and we were like, "We're going to do something". We went and did it and then we came back, and they were like, "We're going to go meet this person." So, I was like, "Okay." And of course, all that happened and occurred. They really didn't tell me anything else. They were like, "We're going to go meet this guy." So, I was like, "Okay."

TEXAS RANGER: Okay. So, what time did you all leave? When you all left before and went and did stuff, what did you all go do?

SAPPHIRE: What did we go do? I'm trying to remember. We were trying to decide on what to eat, and we couldn't find any places to eat. And then we went to Walmart just to look for something. And we couldn't find it. And so, we came back out, and then this is when we came here.

TEXAS RANGER: Okay. So, you all came out here specifically to meet this guy?

SAPPHIRE: I guess so. Like I said, I really don't know what happened. I really don't know. I was just here to follow. That's all. That's really all.

TEXAS RANGER: Okay. All right, we're kind of at the point where you and I both know you're leaving some things out.

SAPPHIRE: No, really, exactly, they were like, "We're going to meet somebody here." I was like, "Okay." I thought it was just a friend of theirs or something.

TEXAS RANGER: Have you ever been out here before for anything?

SAPPHIRE: No.

TEXAS RANGER: Have you ever been out here to do massages, do you even know where you're at right now?

SAPPHIRE: No. Honestly, I don't. I'm not from here.

TEXAS RANGER: Okay. Have you ever been out this way?

SAPPHIRE: I really don't travel around. I stay in the Dallas-Fort Worth area.

TEXAS RANGER: Mm-hmm. Okay.

SAPPHIRE: I'm not leaving anything out. I'm telling you the exact truth.

TEXAS RANGER: Well, the thing is this kind of shit that I'm sitting here looking at right now, this don't just happen. Okay? This happens for a reason.

SAPPHIRE: But they told me that they were going to meet somebody up here. They didn't tell me why. They didn't say anything. They just said, "We're going to meet somebody up here." I thought it was a friend or something. I was like, "Okay." That's exactly what I said.

TEXAS RANGER: Why did you all bring two different cars?

SAPPHIRE: They always roll in different cars. I mean, I don't know.

TEXAS RANGER: Okay. Do you have a car?

SAPPHIRE: No, sir. I do not.

TEXAS RANGER: You don't have one? Okay.

SAPPHIRE: But like I said, that's all I know is that they were like, "Let's meet this person." I was like, "Okay."

TEXAS RANGER: So, about what time did you all leave to come out here? With it being 8:30 pm now and all this stuff happened around 7 o'clock, I believe, or a little before that.

SAPPHIRE: I really don't remember all the time exactly.

TEXAS RANGER: Okay. Did you all drive straight out here?

SAPPHIRE: No. Like I said, we went to go see if we could find anything to eat. We couldn't find anything. We went to Walmart. Couldn't find whatever Jade was looking for. I can't remember what she was looking for. And then we came out here. I don't know after that.

TEXAS RANGER: Okay. So, but when you all left, did you all drive straight here? You didn't stop anywhere?

SAPPHIRE: Yeah, we drove straight here.

TEXAS RANGER: Okay. When you all got here what happened?

SAPPHIRE: When we got here, he pulled up behind our cars, right here and then parked right there. They got in the car. And not even five, ten minutes later, they both got out and he came out with a gun, and he shot Cinnamon and then shot Jade. I don't think he acknowledged that I was here.

TEXAS RANGER: So, he shot, who did he shoot first?

SAPPHIRE: He shot Cinnamon first and then shot Jade.

TEXAS RANGER: Okay. I need you to think back to that, and I know that's probably kind of hard, but I need you to think back to it.

SAPPHIRE: Think back to what?

TEXAS RANGER: To what happened.

SAPPHIRE: That's exactly what happened. I was sitting in the car. I didn't talk to this guy. I did nothing.

TEXAS RANGER: Okay.

SAPPHIRE: I was sitting in the Honda right in the passenger seat. They both got out of the car and went into his car.

TEXAS RANGER: Where did he park?

SAPPHIRE: He parked right beside her car.

TEXAS RANGER: On the left side or the right side?

SAPPHIRE: The left

TEXAS RANGER: Okay.

SAPPHIRE: On the driver's side. And when I looked up, that's when they got, that's when he got out. Cinnamon got out first.

TEXAS RANGER: What door did she get out of?

SAPPHIRE: She got out of the left passenger seat.

TEXAS RANGER: In the back?

SAPPHIRE: In the back seat. Yes.

TEXAS RANGER: So, Cinnamon gets out. What were they doing in the car.

SAPPHIRE: I really don't know what happened in there.

TEXAS RANGER: Left rear. And he shoots her?

SAPPHIRE: Shoots her first. And then Jade gets out, and he's coming around the car and shoots her.

TEXAS RANGER: And where was Jade sitting?

SAPPHIRE: She was sitting in the passenger seat driver's side. Or, yeah, the passenger seat.

TEXAS RANGER: Okay. Then what does he do after he shoots?

SAPPHIRE: He gets in the car and drives off.

TEXAS RANGER: Okay. Which way, how did he pull out of here?

SAPPHIRE: He went around the front, and he drove off that way, south.

TEXAS RANGER: So, he came out this front drive and went south? Okay. So, he passed by you in the vehicle.

SAPPHIRE: I got out into the driver's seat

TEXAS RANGER: After he left?

SAPPHIRE: Yeah, after he left. Because I didn't know whether to call 911 or what just happened.

TEXAS RANGER: Okay.

SAPPHIRE: That's exactly what I did.

TEXAS RANGER: So, did you call 911 eventually?

SAPPHIRE: No, the people in there did. I was like, I don't know what happened. I shook them both to see if they were alive.

TEXAS RANGER: The people in where did?

SAPPHIRE: The man and the woman that called the police.

TEXAS RANGER: Okay.

SAPPHIRE: I'm just as lost as you are because I really don't know what happened.

TEXAS RANGER: Now, Sapphire, I've been doing this for about 22 years. Okay?

SAPPHIRE: Okay, sir.

TEXAS RANGER: And when you told me before that you're scared, I have no doubt that you probably are scared. Okay?

SAPPHIRE: I'm terrified because I really don't know like why a guy would shoot a female. I don't know what happened. You know?

TEXAS RANGER: Uh-huh.

SAPPHIRE: I don't know why he was so crazy. I really don't, sir. Like, do you know what I'm saying?

TEXAS RANGER: And you don't know this guy?

SAPPHIRE: No.

TEXAS RANGER: You don't know who he is at all?

SAPPHIRE: No.

TEXAS RANGER: Okay. You've never seen him before?

SAPPHIRE: No.

TEXAS RANGER: Never seen the vehicle before?

SAPPHIRE: No.

TEXAS RANGER: Speaking of that, what kind of vehicle?

SAPPHIRE: It was a red vehicle. red-maroon vehicle. I don't know exactly what kind, but it was red and maroon. Maroon-looking.

TEXAS RANGER: Was it a sports car?

SAPPHIRE: No, it was just a basic car. He had a white shirt on. He was a white male, and he had like sandy brown hair.

TEXAS RANGER: Okay. All right.

SAPPHIRE: I'm telling you the truth, sir.

TEXAS RANGER: Here's the thing. All you girls live over there with this Cashman. None of you work.

SAPPHIRE: I live with Cashman, but I don't really have anything to do with him.

TEXAS RANGER: Okay. Well.

SAPPHIRE: I don't see anything bad.

TEXAS RANGER: Let me ask you this. Because this whole thing has the look to me like Cinnamon and Jade were into some stuff that they probably shouldn't have been into and were probably dealing with some people that they shouldn't have been dealing with. And my first inclination is that it probably has something to do with drugs. Okay?

SAPPHIRE: With drugs? We don't do drugs. Like, none of us do drugs. I can tell you that right now. None of us do drugs like that. No, sir. I don't think it involved a drug thing. But like I said, I don't know what happened. I wasn't in the car with them to hear the argument or if there was an argument. I don't know.

TEXAS RANGER: Who was it, Cinnamon or Jade, who said, "We need to go meet this guy"?

SAPPHIRE: Both of them. They were like, "We're going to go meet him really quick." And I was like, "Okay."

TEXAS RANGER: Okay. And they didn't say a name at all?

SAPPHIRE: Un-uh.

TEXAS RANGER: They didn't say where.

SAPPHIRE: Un-uh.

TEXAS RANGER: Okay.

SAPPHIRE: I'm telling you the truth

TEXAS RANGER: And yet these girls are going to go all the way out here to come meet somebody that's going to end up blowing both their heads off and running over one of them as he's taking off.

SAPPHIRE: He ran over one of them?

TEXAS RANGER: Yeah. And you all live together, and nobody over there works.

SAPPHIRE: I mean, Cashman—Cashman works.

TEXAS RANGER: Cashman pays for everything

SAPPHIRE: He has his own business. Like, he works.

TEXAS RANGER: Pays for everything. Well, but he's also got a street name of Cashman.

SAPPHIRE: Well, I mean, his whole family calls him that. I mean, I don't, like I said, he doesn't have a street name. He's just, you know, Cashman.

TEXAS RANGER: Cashman. What's the back story to his name?

SAPPHIRE: I don't know.

TEXAS RANGER: Is Cashman into some shit he shouldn't be into?

SAPPHIRE: No, sir. He is not.

TEXAS RANGER: Am I going to find out different when I go check?

SAPPHIRE: No, sir, you won't.

TEXAS RANGER: Do you realize all this stuff that you're telling me is going to get checked out; right?

SAPPHIRE: I know, but sir, this is exactly what happened, I'm telling you the truth. Like, there's nothing going on at the house like that.

TEXAS RANGER: Let's go back to what I told you before.

SAPPHIRE: I know, and I'm telling you the truth though.

TEXAS RANGER: Mm-hmm. Okay.

SAPPHIRE: Like, this is the truth. I don't know why I'm getting in trouble because I'm trying to tell the truth and everyone's mad at me.

TEXAS RANGER: No, you're not getting in trouble. Do I look mad at you?

SAPPHIRE: My friends are dead, I don't know what happened. What am I supposed to do?

TEXAS RANGER: Right now, I need you to tell the truth. I know you are scared. I know you want to help find who did this, right?

SAPPHIRE: Yeah. I do.

TEXAS RANGER: What should happen to this guy after what you just saw him do? What should happen to him?

SAPPHIRE: He should go to jail for a very long time. Like, this is fucked up. Those girls didn't even do anything to him.

TEXAS RANGER: I agree with you. And that's what I'm here trying to do.

SAPPHIRE: I'm figuring it out too, because I'm just as lost as you are. I don't know what happened. I don't. I didn't get in the car with them. I didn't talk to him. I didn't have anything to do with him.

TEXAS RANGER: And you don't know who he is?

SAPPHIRE: No, sir.

TEXAS RANGER: Look, they're not going to get in trouble for anything, obviously, because they are dead.

SAPPHIRE: But, sir, like I said, I don't know.

TEXAS RANGER: Okay.

SAPPHIRE: I'm trying to tell you that's exactly what they told me. I know these girls, but they're not going to exactly tell me what they're doing. I just go with them.

TEXAS RANGER: Okay. let me ask you this. Have they hung around shady people before?

SAPPHIRE: No, sir. Not that I know of.

TEXAS RANGER: You don't just come over and meet somebody and they jump out and pull this kind of shit and then take off and there not be some backstory.

SAPPHIRE: Like I said, I don't know, sir.

TEXAS RANGER: Okay. I'm just going to tell you this, Sapphire. I feel like you're holding something back from me.

SAPPHIRE: But what would it be, though, because I don't know.

TEXAS RANGER: I feel like you're holding something back because you're scared. You just watched this guy kill these two girls; and you're probably thinking, "Shit, if I open my mouth, I'm about to get shot." I mean, let's get real here.

SAPPHIRE: But like I said, though, I don't know why they met him though. I really don't.

TEXAS RANGER: You've got an idea, I think.

SAPPHIRE: I really don't.

TEXAS RANGER: So, you're not holding anything back because you're afraid you're about to be next?

SAPPHIRE: No, I know I'm not going to be next. I felt like, you know, it was my fault or something because I didn't get in the car with them.

TEXAS RANGER: Well, shit. Okay. You didn't get in the car. You didn't get in the car because you didn't know him and you didn't know what was going on, or you didn't get in the car because you were afraid of what they were doing?

SAPPHIRE: I wasn't going to meet him. I didn't talk to him.

TEXAS RANGER: Were you afraid of him? I mean, did you not look… You seem like a pretty streetwise girl. Okay?

SAPPHIRE: Yeah. I thought they knew him, so I didn't have any problem, you know.

TEXAS RANGER: Switch gears back for a second. Do you know anything about Cinnamon or Jade's family and how somebody might be able to get hold of them?

SAPPHIRE: The only person I can think of I would get hold of for the family would be Cashman.

TEXAS RANGER: Okay. Did Cinnamon have a boyfriend?

SAPPHIRE: No, sir. She did not.

TEXAS RANGER: Okay. Did either one of them have boyfriends? I guess Jade is with Cashman; right?

SAPPHIRE: Yeah.

TEXAS RANGER: And Cinnamon doesn't have a boyfriend, this wasn't Cinnamon's crazy ex-husband, boyfriend, anything like that.

SAPPHIRE: No, sir.

TEXAS RANGER: That you know anything about?

SAPPHIRE: No.

TEXAS RANGER: Okay. All right. Is there anything I haven't asked you about this whole thing that you think you need to tell me that's important?

SAPPHIRE: I really do not know what happened. All I know is it happened so fast I had no idea how to react, honestly.

TEXAS RANGER: Mm-hmm.

SAPPHIRE: That guy, I don't know what was said in that car. I don't know what was said in any anything. Do you know what I'm saying? I don't know how this came about, but they said they were going to meet him, so we met him. You know? I'm trying to tell every truth that I can and that's just—I'm scared because I feel like this is my fault I didn't get in the car.

TEXAS RANGER: Does Cashman know what happened?

SAPPHIRE: Yes, I called and told him. *He's here.*

TEXAS RANGER: *I know that,* but I mean, does he know what happened,

SAPPHIRE: No, I don't think he did. like I said, I don't know.

TEXAS RANGER: Okay.

SAPPHIRE: Sir, I really don't.

TEXAS RANGER: What did he say about what happened?

SAPPHIRE: He's devastated. That's all.

TEXAS RANGER: Okay. I told you before that I know you know more, I know you want to help us.

SAPPHIRE: I really do. And I don't know what happened with this. I don't. It escalated so quickly.

TEXAS RANGER: When you were on your way out here, did you talk on the phone to anybody?

SAPPHIRE: No.

TEXAS RANGER: Did you let anybody know where you were going?

SAPPHIRE: No.

TEXAS RANGER: Okay. Did you get any texts or talk to anyone?

SAPPHIRE: No. No.

TEXAS RANGER: I mean, text back and forth?

SAPPHIRE: No, no, no. Nothing, I mean, no.

TEXAS RANGER: What about either one of them?

SAPPHIRE: They talked, we were talking to each other, like, I talked to her. All she said was we're going to go meet this person. I talked to the both of them in person and we got in the car.

TEXAS RANGER: And then all the way out here... You rode out here with Jade. right?

SAPPHIRE: No, I rode out here with Cinnamon.

TEXAS RANGER: With Cinnamon. All the way out here she didn't go into any more detail about why?

SAPPHIRE: No, sir. She didn't. We just turned on the music on and drove here.

TEXAS RANGER: Did she get on the phone and talk to anybody? Is there any little thing you can think of as far as that goes?

SAPPHIRE: Sir, no. *All she (Cinnamon) did was call Jade and ask where she was.* That's it. That's all.

TEXAS RANGER: Okay. And did you all ride out here, like was Jade in front and you all were in the back?

SAPPHIRE: *Jade was in the back, I guess.*

TEXAS RANGER: Who led to this place? Who was in the lead driving here?

SAPPHIRE*: I think Cinnamon was.*

TEXAS RANGER: Okay. So, Cinnamon obviously knew where you were going then; right?

SAPPHIRE: I guess so. Like I said, I don't know what was going on. I really don't. I'm just as clueless as anything. Can I use the restroom?

TEXAS RANGER: Yeah, sure. Hang on. I'll get somebody to run you up there in just a second.

SAPPHIRE: See, sir, I really don't know what happened, and I don't know what escalated in the car for him to shoot them both.

TEXAS RANGER: Okay.

SAPPHIRE: I don't. I mean, whatever it was, I guess it wasn't very good because they got shot. I really need to use the restroom.

TEXAS RANGER: Okay.

SAPPHIRE: That's what happened, sir. I wish I could tell you more.

TEXAS RANGER: Do you have any problem letting me look at the text messages in your phone to make sure you're being totally up front about everything?

SAPPHIRE: Text messages about what?

TEXAS RANGER: About why you were coming out here and any conversation that you might have had with people about why you were coming out here?

SAPPHIRE: I never told anybody I was coming out here.

TEXAS RANGER: You didn't?

SAPPHIRE: No. I'd really like to use the restroom though.

TEXAS RANGER: Okay. So, you don't have any problem showing me your phone if you didn't talk to anybody about anything.

SAPPHIRE: *Sir, no, I'm not going to let you go through my phone.*

TEXAS RANGER: Okay.

SAPPHIRE: That's my information.

TEXAS RANGER: Okay.

SAPPHIRE: But no, I did not tell anybody I was going over here. I didn't say anything. I just really would like to use the restroom if you don't mind. I'm going to pee.

TEXAS RANGER: No. I don't mind you going to pee. But here's the thing. I asked you for consent, but I feel like we've got enough to get a warrant to get into your phone to see what's on there. So, I'm going to take it from you right now.

SAPPHIRE: *Would you please stop?*

TEXAS RANGER: Give me your phone.

SAPPHIRE: Sir, okay. I will but it's locked. Here, I'll unlock it. Okay, I will. Please, okay, I will. Just let it go. Let go of it. I will. I will. I will. Look.

TEXAS RANGER: Are you going to unlock it?

SAPPHIRE: Yes. see, I unlocked it right there.

TEXAS RANGER: All right. Let me have your phone.

SAPPHIRE: I told him where I was.

TEXAS RANGER: Who's telling you to stop talking?

SAPPHIRE: That's his daughter.

TEXAS RANGER: Hang on.

SAPPHIRE: Can I go pee?

TEXAS RANGER: We've got enough to get a search warrant to get into this phone.

SAPPHIRE: Why?

TEXAS RANGER: *Because you're not telling me the truth and you know it.*

SAPPHIRE: Damn it!

TEXAS RANGER: And I'm going to find proof of that on this phone, and you know that, too. Don't you?

SAPPHIRE: No, sir. I don't.

TEXAS RANGER: Yeah, you do.

SAPPHIRE: Because I didn't tell anyone I was coming here. I said where the address was. I sent it to her and I sent it to Nikki. I'll show you everything if you just shut the door, please.

TEXAS RANGER: What are you going to show me?

SAPPHIRE: I'll show you everything. I promise. Just shut the door.

TEXAS RANGER: What are you going to show me?

SAPPHIRE: I'll show you the text messages of the address and everything of what I sent.

TEXAS RANGER: Of what?

SAPPHIRE: Of the address here. That's what I sent Nikki.

TEXAS RANGER: Okay. And…

SAPPHIRE: And I'll show you, yes.

TEXAS RANGER: There's going to be something on the phone.

SAPPHIRE: Babe, I will show you everything if you please give me my phone.

TEXAS RANGER: There's going to be something on this phone here talking about why you all were out here.

SAPPHIRE: No, Babe, it's not. It's really not. Like, I swear to you, it's not. Look, go to the messages over there on the little circle thing. No, it's not in Nikki's thing. I'm telling you where it is. Just shut the door and I'll show you. Look, I'll show you. It's not in there. Look. Go back to the previous messages.

TEXAS RANGER: I'm not letting you touch this phone.

SAPPHIRE: I know. Just put it right here and I'll show you. Okay. Now go to that one. Go to that. See, there's nothing there. All it is just the address of where we were going. That's it, what the address was. I have nothing else, sir, I promise. See, that's Maddie. That's my friend.

TEXAS RANGER: Did you want to come down here and make some money?

SAPPHIRE: And Jade's dad is texting me asking me what's going on. And that's Natalie. She's asking me what's going on. I said that she was shot. "Fucked with the wrong guy," yeah, because the guy came and I was like, "They fucked with the wrong dude. That's the guy that shot them." That's what I'm telling her. Can I please have my phone?

TEXAS RANGER: (Reading text from phone) "I just talked to Cinnamon earlier. He's coming. They

got shot. They're dead. Cinnamon and Jade are dead."
What is that text?

SAPPHIRE: Can I have my phone back, please?

TEXAS RANGER: Is that…

SAPPHIRE: That's just a picture from Instagram that I got and showed her. That's it. I promise. There's nothing else on there. I'm telling the truth.

TEXAS RANGER: Why are people telling you to stop talking?

SAPPHIRE: Because they don't want me to get in trouble. Can I please have my phone back?

TEXAS RANGER: I told you that already. I'm going to get a search warrant.

SAPPHIRE: For no reason. I'm telling you, there's nothing on there. Really, nothing. I showed you. Like, can I please have it back? I won't delete anything. I promise.

TEXAS RANGER: Did you leave?

SAPPHIRE: Leave what?

TEXAS RANGER: Did you leave and come back?

SAPPHIRE: No, sir.

TEXAS RANGER: Well, they're in there watching the video and the black car left after the red one did and then the black car came back. Did you leave and come back?

SAPPHIRE: Yeah, because I didn't know what was going on. Like I'm telling you. I'm scared fucking shitless because I don't know what's going on.

TEXAS RANGER: Mm-hmm. Well, you're also not telling me the truth because you're scared shitless. You know exactly what the hell they were doing over here.

SAPPHIRE: No, really, they were here to meet him.

TEXAS RANGER: I know they were over here to meet him.

SAPPHIRE: But I don't know why they were here to meet him.

TEXAS RANGER: You know why they were here to meet him.

SAPPHIRE: No, sir, I don't.

TEXAS RANGER: These aren't college girls. These aren't little sweet college girls. They got over here and got to dealing with the wrong guy, just like you said in here. And they got their ass killed and you're trying to clam up is what's happening and other people are telling you to clam up.

SAPPHIRE: *If I tell the truth, then what? Then what's going to happen?*

TEXAS RANGER: *If you tell the truth... That means you haven't told the truth.*

SAPPHIRE: No, I'm telling the truth but I'm saying like what if, like what else do you need to know?

TEXAS RANGER: I need to know everything. I need to know who the hell this son of a bitch is. I need to know what they were into.

SAPPHIRE: I really don't know who the guy is.

TEXAS RANGER: Okay.

SAPPHIRE: I really don't.

TEXAS RANGER: Okay. But you know what the hell they were doing over here.

SAPPHIRE: They were here to meet him, but I don't know why.

TEXAS RANGER: They were here to meet him. You know –

SAPPHIRE: No, I really do not know why.

TEXAS RANGER: You know why they were here to meet him.

SAPPHIRE: No, sir, I don't.

TEXAS RANGER: There's talk about drugs and you all live with a guy named Cashman.

SAPPHIRE: But it doesn't mean that we do drugs.

TEXAS RANGER: He's got a street name.

SAPPHIRE: Oh, my god.

TEXAS RANGER: And these girls didn't get killed because some son of a bitch got over here and got pissed off because they brought him the wrong food or whatever.

SAPPHIRE: Sir, I really don't want to get in trouble. I really don't. Am I in trouble?

TEXAS RANGER: You need to start spitting out what happened, you're getting close because you're not telling me the truth.

SAPPHIRE: Okay, sir. Okay, I'll tell you the truth if you please do not get me in trouble. Please, I'll tell you. Just don't get me in trouble. Like, for real.

TEXAS RANGER: I'm ready to write.

SAPPHIRE: You promise you won't get me in trouble? Please protect me. This is why I'm scared. I want to be truthful.

TEXAS RANGER: Okay.

SAPPHIRE: Will you please protect me?

TEXAS RANGER: Yes, I'll protect you.

SAPPHIRE: Okay. What had happened was they told me that they were going to meet this guy. I really don't know why, though; but they said they were going to meet him. They gave me the address and they said they were going to meet him to talk to him about some things. They didn't tell me what it was. I said, :"Okay, cool.". He's like, "I'll meet you over there at the bank." When we came over here, that's when he shot them and stuff. That's when they got in the car. I really, I haven't seen this guy. I really haven't.

TEXAS RANGER: Do Cinnamon and Jade use dope?

SAPPHIRE: No, sir, they don't.

TEXAS RANGER: Do they sling it for somebody else?

SAPPHIRE: No, sir, they don't.

TEXAS RANGER: Okay. What's going on here then? If this is not dope, what it's about? What is it?

SAPPHIRE: I don't know, I really don't know.

TEXAS RANGER: What is about? Are you all prostitutes?

SAPPHIRE: No. I do massages. I don't do prostitution. No.

TEXAS RANGER: Okay. Is Cashman your pimp?

SAPPHIRE: No, sir. He has nothing to do with this.

TEXAS RANGER: Is Cashman your pimp?

SAPPHIRE: No, sir.

TEXAS RANGER: He's not running you all?

SAPPHIRE: No, sir.

TEXAS RANGER: All right. Let's get down to brass tacks. What the fuck happened here tonight?

SAPPHIRE: Like I said, they said they were going to meet this guy and I said, "Okay."

TEXAS RANGER: And they sent you a text?

SAPPHIRE: No, they told me

TEXAS RANGER: They told you

SAPPHIRE: We were all together. Like, "We're going to go meet up with this guy." I said "Okay." So, they texted me. They told me. So, I went over there. We went over there, pretty much, and this is all, I'm telling you.

TEXAS RANGER: No, you're not telling me.

SAPPHIRE: Okay.

TEXAS RANGER: You're not telling me.

SAPPHIRE: They told me when we were at Walmart, "We're going to go meet this guy." I said "Okay." So, we came over here. They texted him and asked him what the address was. He gave them the address. And then from there we came here.

TEXAS RANGER: And you know what they came over here to meet him for and that's the part you're leaving out.

SAPPHIRE: I thought they were just here to talk to him about some things or something. I really don't know exactly what they were here for. I just know they were here to talk to him. Like I said, I don't exactly know what they're here for.

TEXAS RANGER: You ain't keeping anybody out of trouble. They're dead. They already paid for whatever they got into. Okay?

SAPPHIRE: I guess for money. Babe, I really don't know what they were really here for to talk to him about. I've never seen the guy, so I really don't know what they were here to talk to him about. I just know that they were here to meet him for something, and I don't know what it was.

TEXAS RANGER: So, they come to meet a guy that ends up killing both of them.

SAPPHIRE: Yeah, but like I said, I don't know what they came here to meet him for, though.

TEXAS RANGER: Why do you think they came here? You do know what they came here to meet him for.

SAPPHIRE: They could meet him for money. They could meet him for anything. Like I said, I don't know. They said they were here to talk to him.

TEXAS RANGER: Why would they meet him for money?

SAPPHIRE: Like I said, I don't know.

TEXAS RANGER: What were they into? What are you all into?

SAPPHIRE: We do massages. I'm telling you, that's it.

TEXAS RANGER: With a happy ending?

SAPPHIRE: Yeah, happy endings. Yes. There's nothing wrong. Nothing happened. I mean, they told me they called him, they talked to him or whatever, and he would meet us up here. All I said was "Okay." That's it, sir. I swear.

TEXAS RANGER: Mm-hmm.

SAPPHIRE: I'm telling you the truth. We didn't do anything illegal. I promise. There were no drugs involved. We do massages. That's it.

TEXAS RANGER: What were they into that would have got them killed? You know them. You've been living with them.

SAPPHIRE: I'm trying to figure it out. That's what I'm trying to do. I don't know. Cinnamon said she talked to him on the phone a couple of times. "We're going to go meet this guy." I said "Okay." That's all I know. Like, for real. From there on I don't know.

TEXAS RANGER: So, you all three do massages?

SAPPHIRE: Yes, sir.

TEXAS RANGER: And you give a happy ending at the end?

SAPPHIRE: Yes, sir.

TEXAS RANGER: Does that play into this somehow?

SAPPHIRE: I really don't know. about that. I guess they were just here to meet him.

TEXAS RANGER: Does Cashman get a cut of that?

SAPPHIRE: No. It's all of us. Just us three.

TEXAS RANGER: Cashman is fine with his old lady doing that?

SAPPHIRE: I mean, I don't know. I'm not in their business. Like I said, sir.

TEXAS RANGER: Is Cashman running you all? Is that what the deal is?

SAPPHIRE: No, sir. I'm promising you. It's only us three. It was only us three. I promise. I really just don't want to get in trouble. I really don't because this is so stupid.

TEXAS RANGER: Is that what they were supposed to be doing was setting something up?

SAPPHIRE: No, sir.

TEXAS RANGER: Who did you call after you drove off? Did you call Cashman?

SAPPHIRE: I let him know they were dead. Yes.

TEXAS RANGER: Cashman told you not to say anything.

SAPPHIRE: No, that was Nikki, his daughter. I just don't want to get in trouble. I'm trying to tell you everything. And it's bullshit. Now I'm getting my phone searched for nothing and I'm telling you everything. It's just like, we do massages. There's no controlling us whatsoever. It's just us. There's no drugs involved. I don't do drugs. I don't.

TEXAS RANGER: Do you smoke weed?

SAPPHIRE: *Yeah. What's wrong with smoking weed? Is that bad? I guess.*

TEXAS RANGER: *No. I don't necessarily think it's that big of a deal myself either, but are you sure you don't do drugs.*

SAPPHIRE: *No, sir. I don't. I promise I don't.*

TEXAS RANGER: Look, I meant what I said when I sat my ass in here at the very first and I told you not to lie.

SAPPHIRE: Yeah, and I'm telling you the truth though. I don't do drugs. I don't. There's no slinging. There's nothing like that.

TEXAS RANGER: I don't give a rat's ass about any side game, I want to find the son of a bitch.,

SAPPHIRE: I'm telling you, I really don't know who this guy was. I just know what he looked like and that's it.

TEXAS RANGER: I want to find the son of a bitch that killed two damn women. I don't give a shit what they did. They got mixed up with the wrong people.

SAPPHIRE: I know. And I don't know who he is.

TEXAS RANGER: What do you mean by they fucked with the wrong guy?

SAPPHIRE: Like I'm saying, like they got in the car with the wrong guy. That's what I meant. Sir, I promise. Like, that's fucking crazy shit, for real. I don't understand why he would shoot them.

TEXAS RANGER: So that's how you would say they fucked with the wrong guy?

SAPPHIRE: Yeah, like that's the wrong thing to do. You know? They fucked with the wrong guy. That's what I'm saying. I promise.

TEXAS RANGER: How did they fuck with him though?

SAPPHIRE: They got in the car with him.

TEXAS RANGER: Well, that makes me think that you know what they did specifically to piss him off. What did they do?

SAPPHIRE: They could have asked him for money. They could have done anything in that car. They really could have when they went in that car. I didn't see, you know, I didn't know what they were talking about in the car.

TEXAS RANGER: Mm-hmm.

SAPPHIRE: I mean, what else would you like to know so I can tell you? I feel like I'm already in trouble because you have to search my phone.

TEXAS RANGER: Mm-hmm. Where you're going to end up getting in trouble is not telling us the truth or not telling us something that you know which will constitute lying still.

SAPPHIRE: I think they probably gave him a massage and he probably owed them money. You know, like that's all I can think of.

TEXAS RANGER: And Cashman don't know nothing about this?

SAPPHIRE: No,

TEXAS RANGER: Does Cashman know you all give massages?

SAPPHIRE: I guess so. Yes. He does. But he does not run this. It's just us, us three. It was us three. I'm telling you the truth, like everything,

TEXAS RANGER: Did Cashman send you all out here?

SAPPHIRE: No, sir. He did not. I want to go back home. Is there anything else you'd like to know.

TEXAS RANGER: How did you get the address? Did he send it to you?

SAPPHIRE: He sent it, yeah. He sent it and I screenshot it and sent it to Cinnamon.

TEXAS RANGER: So, you don't think we would need to fucking know that because that's got his phone number on it and we could be pinging his damn phone.

SAPPHIRE: Okay, sir, I'm sorry. I really am.

TEXAS RANGER: You don't think that's something important that we need to know?

SAPPHIRE: I'm scared. Like, yes, but I'm scared, though. I don't want to get hurt.

TEXAS RANGER: Who is this guy?

SAPPHIRE: I don't know the guy's name.

TEXAS RANGER: What do they call him?

SAPPHIRE: I don't know. I don't know, honestly. But yeah, they texted, and he texted, and I screenshot and I showed them. I don't know his name.

TEXAS RANGER: Why did he text you?

SAPPHIRE: They told me to text him and to ask him for the number. But it's not on my phone.

TEXAS RANGER: It's not on your phone?

SAPPHIRE: No. It's just a screenshot of it. It was on like a spare phone.

TEXAS RANGER: A what?

SAPPHIRE: A spare phone. Like I had an old phone. I sent it to myself and then like deleted it and then screenshot it and showed it to them. That's what I'm trying to say.

TEXAS RANGER: Where's the old phone?

SAPPHIRE: Not here. It's like at the house. Like I said, I don't know what happened. I don't.

TEXAS RANGER: So, what's on that phone that's going to lead us to him?

SAPPHIRE: *Nothing except the address and his phone number.* I'm telling you the truth on that part. I can even give you his phone number if I can have my phone back.

TEXAS RANGER: You can show us which one it is?

SAPPHIRE: I will. I'm trying to be cooperative. I just don't want to get hurt or anything. I really don't. I'll cooperate. Shit. I'll cooperate.

TEXAS RANGER (to outside person) Hey, bring her phone back over here. The suspect's phone number is in a text message on her phone.

SAPPHIRE: A screenshot. Is there anything else that you would need to know?

TEXAS RANGER: Oh, hell, yeah. I want to know everything you know.

SAPPHIRE: That's what I'm saying.

TEXAS RANGER: You're wanting to get the hell out of here so bad because you're worried that you're going to slip up.

SAPPHIRE: All we do is massages. I really don't know.

TEXAS RANGER: You're worried you're going to slip up, and I get it. Listen, I get what the deal is.

You're probably fucking worried that you're going to end up getting killed because you're not telling me everything. And I can't do shit for you. What's his name?

SAPPHIRE: I don't know his name.

TEXAS RANGER: What do they call him?

SAPPHIRE: I don't know. Sir, I really don't.

TEXAS RANGER: Okay. Are you scared because you think it's going to look like you set this shit up? Is that what you're scared of?

SAPPHIRE: No, I don't want to get called a snitch on some bullshit when I'm not even snitching.

TEXAS RANGER: Snitching?

TEXAS RANGER: Let's get back to why you ended up texting him and all that shit.

SAPPHIRE: Because they told me, they were like, hey, "Text him real quick and ask him for the address."

TEXAS RANGER: Why didn't they just do it?

SAPPHIRE: I don't know. I think they probably did, but I don't know. Like I said, I don't know.

TEXAS RANGER: I mean, if you don't know this guy and you don't know shit about what they're doing, and this is totally this business and all this other shit…

SAPPHIRE: All they asked me was to text him. I said, "Okay," and I did. I texted him to the number right there. That's his number. I just said, "Hey, where do you want to meet us at?" Like, "What's the address?"

TEXAS RANGER: So, they said "Text him"?

SAPPHIRE: They said to text him and say, "What's the address where you are." And so, he texted it.

TEXAS RANGER: So, did they have you do that so he doesn't have you all's real phone number? Is that what the deal is?

SAPPHIRE: I guess so. I don't know. They just told me to text him this number because they didn't want the real number. So, I did. I texted it on the old phone. That's exactly what I did. I screenshot it. I did everything, and I sent it to him and to them.

TEXAS RANGER: Okay. So, then that begs the question, how did they know his number? They gave you his number to text to. Who did that? Which one, Cinnamon or Jade?

SAPPHIRE: Jade. But I don't know how she got his number. I don't know. Like I said, I don't.

TEXAS RANGER: And she said , "Text this guy." and you didn't overhear them talk. I find it hard to believe that throughout all this bullshit you didn't have a damn name, a street name, nothing like that. I mean, I know damn good and well they didn't call him "this guy" all afternoon.

SAPPHIRE: *I'm trying to think of what his name was. Please, hold on. Please. I'm trying to think. Michael. There you go.*

TEXAS RANGER: Where does Michael live?

SAPPHIRE: Sir, I don't know. I really don't.

TEXAS RANGER: How old is he?

SAPPHIRE: I don't know, sir.

TEXAS RANGER: Where does he work?

SAPPHIRE: I don't know, sir.

TEXAS RANGER: What else do you know about him?

SAPPHIRE: That he's crazy and kills people, apparently.

TEXAS RANGER: Who is he?

SAPPHIRE: Like I said, his name is Michael. That's all I know.

TEXAS RANGER: How do you know that?

SAPPHIRE: He told her. I mean, like I said, that's all I know.

TEXAS RANGER: Do you notice, Sapphire, an overriding theme is the longer we talk the more you remember things?

SAPPHIRE: I'm so scared right now, though; you don't get it. Like, I'm fucking terrified.

TEXAS RANGER: Okay. So why don't we take a shit all at once instead of having this constipated kind of conversation?

SAPPHIRE: Okay. Okay. Like, what? Really, what? Like, it's getting my phone searched on some bullshit.

TEXAS RANGER: How does Michael play into this? What was the relationship?

SAPPHIRE: I guess they gave him a massage, sir. I don't know.

TEXAS RANGER: You guess, or is that what happened?

SAPPHIRE: I guess, yes, that's what happened. They gave him a massage. But I don't know why they're coming back for him. I don't.

TEXAS RANGER: So, you've seen him before?

SAPPHIRE: Sir, no. I have not seen this guy.

TEXAS RANGER: How do you know they gave him a massage?

SAPPHIRE: Because that's what we do. Like, I guess that's what happened. I don't know. Oh, man.

TEXAS RANGER: Listen. Make sure you tell me if you're just taking a stab at something or you're telling me what you think, make sure to tell me that, but if you know something tell me that.

SAPPHIRE: I just think that they gave him a massage and he owes them money. That's all I can think of.

TEXAS RANGER: Why do you think that? Something must have happened. You don't just think that something happened.

SAPPHIRE: Babe, I didn't go with them when they did all of this. I don't know. I don't.

TEXAS RANGER: Did they go meet this guy earlier?

SAPPHIRE: No.

TEXAS RANGER: Okay. What did they say about it? They had to have told you something about why they were coming out here to meet him.

SAPPHIRE: Just to talk to him pretty much. They didn't exactly say what they were going to do. They said they were going to talk to him.

TEXAS RANGER: Come on, Sapphire.

SAPPHIRE: No, I'm serious. They said they were going to talk to him. They didn't say what about, but they said they were going to talk to him. I said "Okay." Like, I haven't seen this guy.

TEXAS RANGER: Okay. How do you know they gave him a massage before?

TEXAS RANGER: Medical place. Where is it at?

SAPPHIRE: I don't know exactly where.

TEXAS RANGER: Okay. Where is his place of employment?

SAPPHIRE: Babe, I really, I don't know that part. I really don't. I can't remember.

TEXAS RANGER: Okay. Well, what town is it in?

SAPPHIRE: I don't know either. I can't remember that. It's an hour away from here. That's all I know. I don't know if it's in Fort Worth or it's in Dallas or where.

TEXAS RANGER: Okay. Is that address on your phone?

SAPPHIRE: No, sir.

TEXAS RANGER: Whose phone is it on?

SAPPHIRE: I don't know.

TEXAS RANGER: He had to send you all how to go to there. Who talked to him?

SAPPHIRE: Probably Jade. So, it's probably on her phone.

TEXAS RANGER: So, you and Jade went?

SAPPHIRE: No, it's me and Cinnamon, we went over there and gave him a massage. He gave us money at his place of employment.

TEXAS RANGER: Gave him a massage. Okay.

SAPPHIRE: And we left.

TEXAS RANGER: Where did the massage happen at, inside or in the car?

SAPPHIRE: Inside of his room. Inside of the medical room or whatever.

TEXAS RANGER: Okay. Where was it at?

SAPPHIRE: Honestly, I don't know the location. I don't know all of this. I don't memorize all that.

TEXAS RANGER: How did he get a hold of you all?

SAPPHIRE: He probably called Jade, like I said. I don't remember.

TEXAS RANGER: Okay. Is there some app that you all routinely use? How do people get in contact with you all to get massages?

SAPPHIRE: Vumber.

TEXAS RANGER: That's an app?

SAPPHIRE: Mm-hmm.

TEXAS RANGER: Okay. Did he call your or did he send it to you on Vumber?

SAPPHIRE: I mean, like, she (Jade) controls that stuff. So, no.

TEXAS RANGER: So, Jade is kind of like a boss.

SAPPHIRE: Yes.

TEXAS RANGER: So, you were around this guy. What time was this massage?

SAPPHIRE: Afternoon. Then we left. We did the massage. But there was nothing sexual that happened, I promise. He doesn't get to do anything at all, sexual to us at all.

TEXAS RANGER: So, you're telling me there's no sexual component to these massages at all?

SAPPHIRE: No. None at all.

TEXAS RANGER: Listen, you're not going to get arrested for prostitution; okay?

SAPPHIRE: I know, but I'm telling you, I'm telling you the truth. We do not do anything like that.

TEXAS RANGER: Okay. But I'm telling you that I meant what I said when I sat in here, provided you're honest with me or you don't tell me that you killed somebody, I don't give a shit about drugs or prostitution.

SAPPHIRE: Babe, no, we really don't.

TEXAS RANGER: Okay. Is he a regular customer?

SAPPHIRE: No.

TEXAS RANGER: This is the only time?

SAPPHIRE: This is the only time he ever did this. The only time I've ever seen him.

TEXAS RANGER: How did he find out about you all?

SAPPHIRE: Backpage.

TEXAS RANGER: How do you know that? Is that what he said?

SAPPHIRE: No, we post on Backpage. I think he got our ad, or the ad, whatever.

TEXAS RANGER: Okay. I know a little bit about Backpage but not much, so what's the …

SAPPHIRE: It's got like a massage side and it's got the prostitution side. We post on the massage side.

TEXAS RANGER: So, if I was to go on there to try to find you all, what would I find? What would I look for? What's it called? Is it called something?

SAPPHIRE: I'm trying to think. Not our real names. Cherry. That's the one I can think of.

TEXAS RANGER: All right. So, you and Cinnamon, right, go and give him a massage.

SAPPHIRE: Yes, sir.

TEXAS RANGER: There's more to why a guy that you give a massage would kill two of you.

SAPPHIRE: Like I'm trying to think –

TEXAS RANGER: Well, think hard because I think you know. Or you've got an idea.

SAPPHIRE: That's what I'm trying—like I said, he would owe us money or something, but I don't know.

TEXAS RANGER: Well, how would he owe you money if he paid you $400? I mean, $400 seems like a pretty fair price for an hour and a half, especially with no sex. That's what I meant when I said happy ending a while ago.

SAPPHIRE: I'm just trying to think of why they would go back to him. That's what I'm trying to think. I don't know. I've seen the guy, but he wasn't going to go crazy on me though. *He didn't go crazy when we saw him. He really didn't. He seemed normal.*

TEXAS RANGER: What, yesterday?

SAPPHIRE: Yeah. There was nothing wrong yesterday.

TEXAS RANGER: Okay. I need you to think real hard about where in the hell you all went. Where this massage took place. Okay,

SAPPHIRE: If I had my purse I would have had like his card.

TEXAS RANGER: Where is your purse?

SAPPHIRE: It's in the Honda over there. I think I have his card in there with the location of where it's at.

TEXAS RANGER: And it's got his business stuff on it?

SAPPHIRE: Yes, sir.

TEXAS RANGER: I mean, you spent an hour and a half massaging him. You probably know what he looks like. It was just yesterday.

SAPPHIRE: Yeah, I'm scared, really. I don't know why they came back over here and talked to him. I really don't. I mean, we got the money. I mean, other than that, I don't know why they would have come back over here unless, hey, I want some more money.

TEXAS RANGER: Come on, Sapphire.

SAPPHIRE: I'm really thinking that because that's the only thing is, they wanted some more money.

TEXAS RANGER: Do you want some gum?

SAPPHIRE: I would really like my phone back.

TEXAS RANGER: Well, that shit isn't happening.

SAPPHIRE: When will I get it back?

TEXAS RANGER: Well, probably here as soon as we get done dumping everything, we need out of it. I'm not going to keep it from you forever.

SAPPHIRE: I mean, I'm trying to cooperate and give as much information as I can.

TEXAS RANGER: *We had to drag this shit out of you kicking and screaming. And I get that you're freaked out. I mean, even now after I know that you've lied to me and withheld shit, I'm not inclined to handcuff you and tell you you're going to jail. I'm giving you a little bit of understanding for what you just went through. You're probably shitting your pants. I get that. Okay,*

SAPPHIRE: I got my phone taken because you all think that I'm up to something, and I'm really not.

TEXAS RANGER: You were right here when it happened. Two women got killed. *Look, I've been doing this for 21 years. I knew this shit wasn't adding up and you weren't telling us everything.*

SAPPHIRE: We just do massages. And I don't understand why that guy flipped out on them like that.

TEXAS RANGER: Okay. Well, let's get to that. Yesterday at this massage… About how old is this dude?

SAPPHIRE: He's like 36—36-ish.

TEXAS RANGER: Is that what he told you or –

SAPPHIRE: No, it's just I'm estimating.

TEXAS RANGER: Okay. All right. Describe him for me.

SAPPHIRE: *He's kind of tall, shortish, chubby.*

TEXAS RANGER: *Tall, shortish, chubby. Wait a minute! Is he tall or short?*

SAPPHIRE: He's like in between.

TEXAS RANGER: So, just like regular height?

SAPPHIRE: Mm-hmm. He's chubby. He's white. *He has brown eyes.*

TEXAS RANGER: Chubby, brown eyes?

(Texas Ranger obtains card from purse)

TEXAS RANGER: *It's been like trying to pull sunshine out of a cat's ass to get you to tell me what's up. I realize you're worried about getting in trouble. All these other thoughts that are going through your head and everything. But the fact of the matter is you watched this guy kill two friends of yours and it took me three hours to get information from you.*

(Interview ends)

Well, now, that was something. It took the Texas Ranger over three hours to pull information from

Sapphire. I know the crime boss and his daughter and everyone else she contacted told her not to say anything, and she really followed their orders; but if you dig in the sewer long enough, you're bound to pull something out. Like the Texas Ranger stated, it was "like pulling sunshine out of a cat's ass." As you will find in later chapters Sapphire never really told the Texas Ranger all the truth about her full involvement in this matter. They never gave Michael a massage, they never intended to give Michael a massage. Once they have their mark, they never stop going after them, as long as they're alive, anyway.

Chapter 7
Who's the lead Detective

Let's see if we can determine who was in charge of this nightmare. The crime boss, Cashman was at the crime scene. Could he have been the fourth person that arrived with Sapphire, Jade, and Cinnamon that evening, the fourth person that law enforcement never looked for? He was never interviewed and never investigated. We know that Cashman spearheaded this organized crime group, regardless of how hard Sapphire tried to cover for him. I would be afraid too if I said something to implicate the head of this organized crime group. We know that he has been prosecuted twice by the federal government for similar activity. He used a "bottom bitch" like Jade to do his bidding; and in those prosecutions, he cut deals and pled guilty. The District Attorney is this case fought tooth and nail to successfully keep him out of the courtroom at Michael's trial and protected him at all costs. On that November night in 2017, was there a conspiracy brewing, a conspiracy to prosecute a man for exercising his right to self-defense against an organized crime boss?

Consider the most experienced investigator in the county, highly trained in criminal investigations, similar to FBI agents, a Texas Ranger with 20 plus years of experience. He conducted the interviews of

Sapphire and Michael, he accepted evidence and submitted it to the state crime lab, he seemed to be in charge; but no, he stated that he was not in charge of the investigation.

Then there is the lead detective. She did not interview anyone. She was not the arresting officer. She was not even present during the arrest and execution of the search warrant. The police website lists her official title as Sergeant of Support Services. *"The Support Services Division provides internal support to the various divisions within the department, in addition to assisting the public with police reports and property management/recovery."* We know that she was in charge of the evidence, the evidence that had no chain of custody. We also know she was not a detective and she had never worked on a homicide case. The defendant's vehicle was towed from the home without an officer maintaining chain of custody. Who knows what really happened after it was towed away? Sgt. Smith did even not know many facts of the case and could not recall facts and evidence at trial.

Several law enforcement officers were called to testify at trial, including the Texas Ranger; and all of them stated that they were not in charge of the investigation and did not know who was. Take a moment and picture yourself in a courtroom where you're on trial for your life, and all the law enforcement officers tell the entire courtroom under oath that they were not in charge of the investigation and do not know who was. It's only your life they are trying to take away. What do they mean no-one knows who was in charge?

After they had questioned Sgt. Smith in court, she was "retained" for later questioning. Then, all of a sudden, after a short meeting with Sgt. Smith and the prosecution, the prosecutor called her back to the stand. Now she states that she guesses she was in charge. Oh my! She walked into the court room with a paper bag that had never been sealed which contained evidence, including the large bag that Cinnamon carried on her shoulder. The bag was not in any container to prevent evidence tampering, and all the evidence was handled with no gloves! Smith stated, "I was in charge of the evidence, it was our case and our scene."

She never talked to the witness, never talked to the 911 caller, never talked to Michael. She did work with Ms. Mann to coauthor a criminal affidavit stating facts that she only had vague hearsay knowledge of. She worked with the untrained, unlicensed, uncertified CSI person to get an arrest warrant and search warrants. So, at the end of the prosecution's questioning, Smith claimed to have been in charge, but who was really in charge? Was anyone in charge? Was Cashman and his influence in charge?

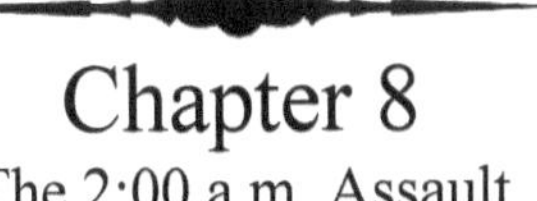

Chapter 8
The 2:00 a.m. Assault

It's around 2:00 a.m., and Michael's dad's phone begins to ring, Michael's mom at first just pushed cancel, thinking no-one should be calling at 2:00 a.m. Then the phone rings again.

The caller on the other end said, "This is the Sheriff's Department. We need everyone in the house to come out of the house NOW, with your hands in the air."

Michael's mom told his dad, "The police are outside and ordered us all to come out, get up NOW."

She then went to get everyone else up. As she walked through the family room and into the foyer, she was blinded by a very bright light shining through all the front windows and could also hear the bullhorn speakers from the police units blaring out, "Everyone in the home come out now with your hands up, you have two minutes before we enter the home by force."

The announcement was stated repeatedly. As she approached the front door, Michael walked out the front door first with his hands high in the air. He stated, "I am the one you're looking for."

Michael's Mom could hear the police yelling commands at her son, Michael, and oh my goodness, so many police officers pointing guns at him, unnecessarily forcibly pushing him to the ground holding guns literally up against his head and cursing at him as they gave him commands. Michael fully complied with all the officer's commands and did not resist their orders at all. At this point, all she could do was to continue to make sure everyone else was awake and coming out. Everyone began to walk out the door one at a time. Michael's wife and his then teenage daughter both were targeted by laser sights from SWAT assault teams and snipers on the neighbors' rooftops. Michael's Mom was also targeted by laser sights and greeted by police pointing weapons in her face. She was patted down, handcuffed, and told to sit on the curb across the street. The next one out was Michael's little brother only 15 years old. He was targeted by snipers on the rooftops, and officers aggressively ran up to him and put a gun barrel directly to his head and told him to get the fuck on the ground. Then they gave him an assist, throwing him on the ground and then handcuffing him. The last person out was Michael's dad. Michael's dad at the time worked with another law enforcement agency in the area — that's why they called his cell phone that morning. When he walked out of the home, police officers told him to put his hands where they could see them, and he complied. No-one rushed over and put a gun to his head or threw him on the ground; but, of course, he was not small and fragile like the women and children.

He walked all the way to the curb where everyone was sitting, and then the officers came over and stated, "We are going to place you in handcuffs, okay?"

Then, a dozen officers, went into the home to conduct a search. They did not show anyone a search warrant at this time and would not tell anyone a reason as to why the family was being detained. So, there we all sat on a cold November morning, wearing only what we had on when we went to bed the night before. Michael's dad had on a pair of socks and took them off to give to Michael's mom so she would not be barefoot in the cold. No-one was allowed into to the house to get a jacket or even to use the bathroom for hours as they conducted a search of the home. Although Michael's mom was having trouble breathing, she was too afraid to even ask to get her medicine. You just don't do that with people pointing guns at your head. The women and children were shaking from the cold, sitting on a cold cement curb, and no-one would tell them what this was all about. Michael had been placed in the back of a police vehicle, and the vehicle had pulled away from the home. A tow truck pulled up to the home and backed up to Michael's vehicle and began to hook up to Michael's vehicle. Michael's dad asked the tow truck driver if he was going to use tow dollies on the front tires as not doing so could damage the vehicle's transmission. The tow truck driver would not respond to Michael's dad, so Michael's dad went over and asked the Texas Ranger.

The Texas Ranger stated, "You will have to ask the County guys, they are running this investigation, not me."

So, Michael's dad went to the County detectives and asked if they could get the tow truck driver to use tow dollies so they would not damage the driveway and/or the vehicle. One of the county detectives said, "You have bigger problems to worry about right now than that."

No surprise, the tow truck driver hooked a cable to Michael's vehicle and drug it out of the driveway and onto the tow truck with the tires dragging all the way. Then the Texas Ranger and the county detectives talked to Michael's dad.

The detectives stated, "Your son has been charged with capital murder."

In his head, Michael's dad was thinking "What the hell? They have made a terrible mistake."

The detective continued to tell Michael's dad that Michael was being booked into the county jail and the family should be able to talk to him later that day. The detective then asked Michael's dad if he had any questions, and his dad replied that he did not but asked for a copy of the search warrant and a list of items they took from his home.

The detective stated, "It's on the dining room table" and turned and walked away saying, "You can now return to your home."

This was shortly after 6:00 a.m.

Chapter 9
What's Next

Michael's dad called the family to the dining room table. Everyone was pretty much still in shock, cold, upset that Michael had been arrested, and just physically and mentally drained. Michael's dad and mom went right to work. His dad grabbed his computer and started looking for attorneys. It was early Sunday morning, but they knew the most important thing to do right away was to get an attorney there as fast as possible and tell Michael to invoke his right to remain silent. Michael's dad knew that police will do almost anything to get a confession and that any little thing you say will be twisted and used against you in court. So, Michael's dad was looking up lawyers and calling out numbers to Michael's mom, who was calling the attorneys. Finally, an attorney answered the phone and said he would go and meet Michael that morning. Typically, when you tell an attorney the charge is capital murder, the beginning price is $500,000 just to talk to you.

Well, the attorney agreed to meet with Michael and advise him of his right to remain silent and to pass a message to him "Do not say anything, let your attorney speak for you." He agreed only to charge $2,000 up-front just for the one-time meeting. The lawyer went and met with Michael in the county jail and told Michael not to say any more than he already had and not to talk to anyone but him about what happened, and they proceeded to discuss why he was arrested.

Michael's mom and dad met with the attorney on the following Tuesday to discuss the case, and the attorney explained that Michael was charged with capital murder of multiple persons and that that charge could carry the "DEATH PENALTY." Quietly, Michael's mom and dad were overcome with panic but remained as calm as possible.

Dad stated, "Michael? No, they have the wrong guy. Michael could not hit the broad side of a barn with a gun."

The attorney just nodded his head and restated that was what he was charged with. The attorney then stated that the money he had been paid was just for the Sunday visit but did not retain him for this case, and so began the "Money Talk."

Michael's mom and dad had done some research on the Internet about the attorney, and he had a great resume. The attorney stated that he would take Michael's case if they chose to hire him.

He also stated, "Make no mistake, you may be paying the bill, but Michael is my client, and I can only release information that he authorizes me to release."

Of course, they agreed to the attorney contract, and Michael's dad signed it. Then, the attorney took the contract to Michael in county jail and had him sign it as well. So, the ball was started rolling, with Michael's family thinking this matter would get resolved quickly.

Michael's mom and dad and wife met with the attorney again around about a week later. Michael had told the attorney not to hold any information back from them but to tell them everything. You could have heard a pin drop on a soft pillow when the attorney told everyone that Michael had had to shoot the two women in self-defense. The attorney stated that they were trying to force Michael into their vehicle and threating to kill him and his family.

Everyone left the attorney's office in shock; and it was a long, quiet ride home. When they got home, his dad said, "Okay, the attorney said this was self-defense. We will continue to stand with Michael. This was not cold-blooded murder. The attorney got the whole story from Michael, and he did it to save his life and ours as well."

Everyone agreed to stand with and support Michael, and Michael's dad told everyone not to discuss anything with anyone outside the home.

While his family was busy getting a lawyer, Michael was put in a solitary cell with nothing on but a small paper gown. Water leaked into the cell, and it was very cold. They would not even give him a blanket.

Although the detective had said the family would be able to visit Michael later in the day that he was arrested, that turned out not to be true. Michael was not allowed to have a visitor or even a call with anyone other than his attorney until the end of the week. Michael was kept in solitary confinement for 33 days. He did not get recreation, tv, books, nothing but a small cell for 33 days.

Michael's dad had had enough, so he sent a complaint to the state prison commission stating that Michael's rights were being violated. Within 2 days the warden called and wanted to meet with Michael's dad, so Michael's mom and dad went to meet the warden. The warden was very courteous and gave them a tour of the jail. Then they went into his office. He stated that he was protecting Michael by keeping him separated from other inmates who might be part of the organized crime organization. Dad thanked him for helping protect Michael but stated to keep him locked in a small cell with no recreation time and poor conditions was abusive. The warden stated that he did not realize that Michael was not getting any recreation time and that he would get that corrected right away. The same day after the meeting with the warden, Michael was moved to a room with three other inmates. That cell had a television, he began to get his recreation time regularly, and life became a little more bearable for Michael. Meanwhile, Michael's mom and dad had been pushing the attorney to request a bond hearing since at that point there had not been a bond set. Of course, Michael also had not yet been indicted, just held in the county jail with no bond. So, about 65 days after Michael's arrest, the district attorney brought the case to a grand jury and indicted him. Then, a bond hearing was finally held. Michael's bond was set at $400,000.

Michael's mom and dad then had to search for a bail bondsman. You would think this would be easy, but his mom and dad found out that in a capital murder case getting a bond was as hard as or harder than getting an attorney. His mom and dad called everyone they could find, with no luck. One bondsman stated he would put up the bond for a fee of $400,000 and having ten people to guarantee the bond. His dad's response was, "If I had $400,000, I would post a cash bond."

Finally, Michael's mom and dad called the last bondsman on the list. The bondsman stated he would consider posting the bond, but he wanted to meet with Michael's parents in person first. They gladly agreed and met with him the next morning. After asking them several questions, the bondsman told them he wanted to check a few things out and he would call them later. Michael's mom and dad were on pins and needles as they waited to hear back from the bondsman.

To try to get their minds off the situation while they waited, they went to a movie. They all pretended to watch the movie, but let's face it, they didn't care about a movie. When Michael's dad got a call from the bondsman in the middle of the movie, he stepped out to take the call. The bondsman said to be at the jail about 4:00 p.m., that they were in the process of making Michael's bond and he should be ready by 4:00 p.m. and to bring him directly to their office to pay the bond amount and sign contracts. Michael's dad was so overwhelmed with this blessing from God that he could hardly get out the words to respond, but he took a breath and thanked him and stated they would follow his instructions to the letter. Michael's dad had to take a moment and catch his breath and compose himself before telling Michael's mom and little brother, and they all sighed a huge sigh of relief. They did not say anything to anyone and followed the instructions from the bondsman's office. After 66 days in county jail, Michael was again breathing free air.

His mom and dad took him to get something to eat and let him prepare for coming home after 66 days in jail. They had Michael walk into the house and wait in the living room. Then they called Michael's daughter to come downstairs. When she walked into the room and saw Michael standing there, she ran to Michael, crying, and held him for at least 20 minutes and would not let go. Michael's dad and mom were happy that the family was back together, but they also knew this is just the beginning and there would be many ups and downs along the way. However, nothing, not even his dad's experience with law enforcement, could prepare them for what was ahead of them all.

Chapter 10
The Mystery Phone

Several days after that fateful night in November, another law enforcement agency and the fire department were working an accident about five miles away from where Michael had shot Cinnamon and Jade in self-defense. It was a cold day, and it had been raining on and off for a couple of days. Outside ambient temperature was below 40 degrees. The wet weather is most likely what contributed to the multiple motor vehicle accident that happened on the interstate.

While working the accident, the fire department Operations Chief was looking for debris from the vehicles involved in the accident and noticed a cell phone laying in a puddle of water along with what appeared to be scattered parts of another phone. He pulled the phone from the puddle of water; and oddly enough, the phone was still on and, by official reports, almost fully charged. He took it to an officer on the scene. Oddly, neither the fire department Operations Chief nor any of the officers on the scene asked if the phone happened to belong to anyone at the scene of the accident, even though there is usually a lot of paperwork involved in putting a phone into evidence and especially accessing a phone for information.

The officer testified that he placed the phone in his vehicle to bring back to the police station to place it in evidence as found property. At the police station, the officer tagged the phone to be put into evidence. He then began looking at the contents of the phone and even made a call to a number saved in the phone. That was none other than Nikki (Cashman's daughter). Nikki told the officer that it was her phone and asked what he was doing with it and demanded the officer return the phone to her immediately. Nikki then told the officer that her "sister" (Jade) had been killed a few days before and that she must have had the phone with her. The officer told Nikki that he would be putting the phone into evidence, and she would have to contact detectives.

Now, I feel I must point out a very important fact here. The phone had been left outside, submerged in water, in cold weather, and not hooked up to a charger for several days. How does any phone retain a battery for that long? Not to mention being submerged in water and still operational.

Anyway, the cell phone in question was turned on when the Operations Chief discovered it. It had been submerged in a puddle of water with an ambient temperature below 40 degrees for several days "supposedly." It could have been a lost or discarded phone or may have belonged to someone at the accident scene; but the fire department Operations Chief did not ask anyone if the phone was theirs, nor did any of the law enforcement officers. Why did they not ask the motorists involved in the accident if the cell phone belonged to anyone there? That would seem to be what a reasonable person would have asked if they found property laying in a ditch at an accident scene. No, the officer put the phone in his vehicle then put it in the evidence room as found property. Did they already know the phone did not belong to any of the motorists at the scene? And if they did know, how did they know, and why are they telling such an elaborate story? Was it part of their determination to build up a case against Michael and protect the crime boss? Did they really find a phone submerged in a puddle of water in a ditch on the side of the highway?

Now, although police are almost never allowed to search your cell phone without a warrant or explicit permission, they may be able to do so in certain emergency situations. There was no emergency at that time. The Supreme Court of the United States has ruled that a warrantless search can be justified under "exigent circumstances." Usually, this requires that the police have probable cause and a lack of time to secure a warrant to prevent imminent danger to life or the destruction of evidence. If the police believe that your phone holds key evidence that is time-sensitive and could potentially put lives in danger – such as in the case of a kidnapping or bomb threat – they can claim that exigent circumstances required them to search your phone without a warrant. The officer never applied for or received a search warrant, and there was certainly no emergency situation at the time.

The mystery phone story... Will we ever find the truth? When court begins, the District Attorney claims that Michael tossed the phone there following the shooting. Apparently, he believes that this cell phone was submerged in a puddle of water in cold weather for five days but still worked and even had a full battery charge. But wait. It gets even crazier. The District Attorney sent the phone to the State of Texas Crime Lab for DNA tests.

When asked for an update on the case by a local reporter on January 4, 2019, the District Attorney stated, "We are waiting on the results of the DNA tests."

The phone was found in November 2017, and the District Attorney wants everyone to believe he was still waiting on the DNA results in January 2019. When the District Attorney finally had to share the results of the DNA tests, they showed that Michael was excluded from the phone as his DNA was not found on the phone. Michael had nothing to do with the cell phone supposedly found at the accident scene. It gets better. DNA from Jade and Cinnamon was on the phone, as well as DNA from two other unknown persons. Of course, they never tested DNA for Sapphire, Cashman, or Nikki, even after the two unknowns were discovered by the crime lab. The District Attorney did not care to follow the evidence and did not care about the truth. The District Attorney to this day has no idea who the two unknown people are who left DNA evidence on the mystery phone, and he does not want to find them. Or does he know and is protecting them while lying to build his case against Michael?

Chapter 11
The District Attorney

This very well-educated man graduated with honors with a Bachelor of Science double major in Political Science and Radio-TV-Film. That's right – he knows how to put on a show. He graduated from law school less than two years later. After passing the Texas bar examination, he became a licensed attorney and began his legal career as an Assistant County Attorney in a rural county. After two years of handling misdemeanor offenses, he then moved to the County District Attorney's Office. In November 2017, he was still an Assistant District Attorney. About a year before the trial, he was elected District Attorney.

This District Attorney refused to charge Sapphire with her known crimes of aggravated robbery with a deadly weapon, kidnapping, forced entry, terroristic threats to commit bodily harm and traffic a minor into the sex trade. He refused to investigate Cashman for the organized crime activities that his organization was actively involved in against Michael and thousands of other victims. No, he chose to protect Cashman and his organization at all costs, including blatantly lying and misleading to the jury throughout the trial.

As I said, this man focuses on putting on a show. So, it should be no surprise that he had to be admonished by the judge during the trial for talking about the case outside of the jury room with jurors standing nearby. That probably should have been a mistrial, but not in this rural county in Texas. He also used the "Golden Rule" argument, which is generally considered unethical. The "Golden Rule" asks the jury to put themselves in the place of the "victim" and to imagine a situation with a different outcome. For example, imagine that Cinnamon went to jail for a few years, "found God," had a family, and was working hard at fast food because that was the only job she could get. Obviously, this biases the jury. There seems to be no limits to what this District Attorney would do to protect this organized crime organization and all its participants. The question is, why?

Now for a little bit of background on Texas law. Self Defense law in Texas is very specific:

"A person is justified in using force against another when and to the degree the person reasonably believes the force is immediately necessary to protect that person against the other's use or attempted use of unlawful force. The person's belief that the force was immediately necessary as described by this subsection is presumed to be reasonable if the person: knew or had reason to believe that the person against whom the force was used: unlawfully and with force entered, or was attempting to enter unlawfully and with force, the person's occupied habitation, vehicle, or place of business or employment; unlawfully and with force removed,

or was attempting to remove unlawfully and with force, the person from the person's habitation, vehicle, or place of business or employment; or was committing or attempting to commit aggravated kidnapping, murder, sexual assault, aggravated sexual assault, robbery, or aggravated robbery. A person is justified in using deadly force against another to protect land or tangible, movable property: if he would be justified in using force against the other under Section 9.41; and when and to the degree he reasonably believes the deadly force is immediately necessary: to prevent the other's imminent commission of arson, burglary, robbery, aggravated robbery, theft during the nighttime, or criminal mischief during the nighttime; or to prevent the other who is fleeing immediately after committing burglary, robbery, aggravated robbery, or theft during the nighttime from escaping with the property."

If the District Attorney had actually read the Texas penal code and followed the laws written and passed by the Texas legislators, by this point we have seen enough information just from the witness statement from Sapphire that this case should have been dismissed.

Sadly, no such luck. This District Attorney appears to be conspiring to protect the entire organized crime group. One can only speculate as to why would a District Attorney go to such lengths to protect such a vile organization. I, for one, am puzzled. Why does organized crime continue to go unchecked and unprosecuted in this District Attorney's jurisdiction?

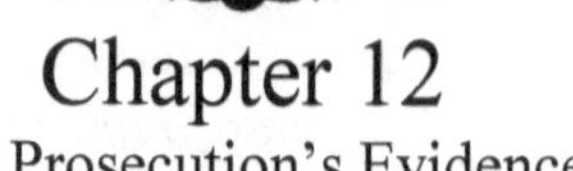

Chapter 12
The Prosecution's Evidence

Let's take a quick at what evidence the District Attorney will be bringing to court to justify the charge of Capital Murder against Michael. Just think about that charge of Capital Murder. That charge comes automatically with a minimum sentence of Life in Prison Without the Possibility of Parole but can even be Death.

Everyone should take a pause and really consider the evidence and all the circumstances involved before and during the incident before taking someone's life away. Don't make the mistake of thinking life in prison without the possibility of parole is not taking away a young man's life. He will still die in the prison. He just may have to live there for many years of suffering before that happens.

At this point, the District Attorney knows that Michael will be claiming self-defense and will be taking the stand in court to explain his actions that night and why he had to resort to using deadly force. What evidence could the District Attorney bring to court to dispute Michael's claim of self-defense? Michael did not call 911 or go to the police right away. He hid the gun that night in some brush. He went and put fuel in his vehicle and went through an automatic car wash. He had contacted this organization for an erotic massage to begin with, not knowing it was an organized crime syndicate. He was robbed and kidnapped the day before and yet again did not call the police. He did shoot two people, resulting in their deaths.

The District Attorney will say that Michael dumped the mystery phone out his window on the way home that night. He will continue this fabrication of the truth, knowing full well he is lying to the jury.

The Texas Ranger sent many pieces of evidence to the Texas crime lab for analysis, but only 10 items were tested. Only 10 Items were considered to be associated with this incident.

The District Attorney will say to the jury that the crime scene investigator and detectives found hair in the wheel well of Michael's vehicle just before the early morning raid on the family home. The analyst from the state crime lab stated the hair received was from the undercarriage, not the wheel well, and they did not run DNA tests on the hair sample as it did not appear to be human hair.

That mystery phone keeps coming up, even though Michael was excluded from ever touching it, but you would think it was the holy grail of evidence. This District Attorney will continue to ignore the truth and the evidence from the Texas crime lab analyst. He will continue the lie and keep insisting that Michael tossed it on his way home that evening.

Now, we can see the evidence. Michael was scared, confused, and in shock after the shooting and made some bad decisions afterwards that a reasonable person in a normal situation may not have made. This was not a normal situation. The law states that it does not matter what he did afterward. He used deadly force in self-defense. The only thing the jury is to consider is the facts leading up to the incident and the reasons for using deadly force, if Michael was justified in the use of deadly force, any mistakes he made after he left the scene do not matter. Michael was charged with capital murder but never charged evidence tampering, so the only consideration was whether it was justified self-defense or murder.

Remember the Texas Penal code: "The person's belief that the force was immediately necessary as described by this subsection is *presumed to be reasonable if the person: was being robbed, kidnapped, felt his life was in danger, multiple assailants.*" Really, the only evidence the District Attorney brought was that these women committed vile crimes thousands of times per year throughout the United States. But he fabricated stories to mislead the jury with fairy tales and lies.

That in a nutshell is what is anticipated. This is not a who-done-it case. Michael was in a situation where he had to protect himself and his family. The case should be determined by the justification to use deadly force, but can Michael expect a fair trial from this rural area District Attorney and small-town justice? It's not looking good at this point.

Chapter 13
The Defendant

Michael is in his early thirties. He is married to Lacy and has one child. His wife Lacy was married once before and had a daughter. When Michael married her, he adopted her daughter as well. His daughter's birth father was a convicted sex offender and was on parole when Michael met his soon-to-be wife, but a few years later Lacy's ex-husband traveled to another state with a plan to abuse a 10-year-old child and was arrested and prosecuted. Michael stepped up and helped Lacy fight to get the birth father's parental rights revoked and then adopted Lacy's daughter as his own. Michael loves his daughter dearly, and there is nothing he wouldn't do to care for and protect his daughter, just like any other father would do.

Michael had a normal childhood, growing up in a middle-class family. Michael's mom and dad taught him the four most important things in life to always remember—God, family, country, and work. Michael played sports in school and participated in activities in church. He loved the church camps every summer. He always said it was an awesome time for reflection and to be with God. He graduated high school with honors and went to college to study nursing. Michael always wanted to help others. He really always had a servant's heart. If anyone ever asked him for his help, he never hesitated—he was there for them. After graduating college and passing the state board of nursing exam, he was immediately hired by a large hospital in the area.

As I said, Michael always wanted to help others in need; and he felt he could accomplish this by being both a nurse and working in an administrative role at the hospital. In the administrative role, Michael could develop programs to help in mental health and the underserved communities, and he did just that.

Michael's marriage to Lacy was one most people would describe as toxic and unhealthy. Lacy was from a broken home and raised by relatives at times and by foster parents at other times. Before Michael met Lacy, she had been living out of her vehicle, doing whatever she could to make it on the streets. Lacy had worked as a stripper in the past before Michael met her. She sent Michael a friend request through social media. They began correspondence with each other for a while before they met. One thing led to another, and Michael let Lacy move into his apartment since she was basically living out of her car. After a few months of living together, Michael proposed, and Lacy accepted. They seemed to be good together at first, but then there were the affairs. Even after they got married, Lacy would make dates with other men and have affairs. Michael was hurt and at times devastated, but he always found a way to forgive Lacy for being unfaithful to him.

Michael and Lacy continued to plan their wedding, and Michael wanted everything to be perfect for Lacy. He made sure she would get the fairytale wedding she dreamed of. He planned their honeymoon at Disney, California, just like she had always wanted.

The big wedding and reception with all their friends and family was completed with a honeymoon to California and a trip to Disney and more. But, the day after their return, and I mean the day after they returned from their honeymoon, Lacy told Michael she was going to her friend's house a few miles away to visit. Well, that wasn't quite the truth. She pulled an all-night party with her friends; and yes, I think there were more guys than girls at this party. The next morning Lacy come in the door looking like she had been dragged through a field and covered in bug bites. Michael took his wedding vows very seriously and always forgave her. I am not so sure I could be that forgiving. He even worked to help her eventually get enrolled into a local college for some classes. He wanted to make sure she had every opportunity to succeed in life just like he had. Lacy could not quite understand or accept the blessing that comes with a close family relationship and the support of caring parents. She always resisted going to family events with Michael and tried to keep him from going as well.

This behavior continued throughout their marriage until they divorced in 2021. Lacy had decided to spend a month or so with an old boyfriend; and when she returned home, she told Michael she just could not stand him anymore and wanted a divorce. He agreed. Michael sold their home and split all the proceeds between Lacy and his daughter, taking nothing for himself. He rented a storage unit and moved all the furnishings and appliances into there for Lacy. When the divorce was complete, Lacy received all the furnishings from their home and two-thirds of the proceeds from the sale of the home, and Michael gave the other one-third of the proceeds to their daughter. Michael only kept his clothes and moved in with his mom and dad.

You can come to your own opinion about Michael, but anyone who knows him—friends, family, business associates—will all say he is a kind, gentle, caring, and charitable man. Of course, like most men or women, you'd better not threaten to harm and or traffic his children or his family.

━━━◆◆◆◆━━━

Chapter 14
The Trial Begins

et's do a little housekeeping. Once Michael was arrested, he was kept in jail for over two months before a bond hearing was allowed. Then, when he was finally able to be bonded out, he had to wear a GPS monitor and report to a county probation officer weekly and be subjected to random drug testing. His costs and fees for monitoring, etc., exceeded over $500 per month, not to mention time off work. Michael was subjected to this continuously for over four and a half years, with costs that exceeded more than $20,000, not including attorney fees and the cost for the bond.

The first notice of trial was in July 2019. That was just too fast for the District Attorney, so they asked for a continuance.

The second notice of trial was in April 2020. The judge got COVID, so it was reset.

The third notice of trial was in August 2020. The District Attorney asked for a continuance due to COVID-19. This request was two days before the trial.

The fourth notice of trial was in September 2021. A witness had to have surgery, so another continuance was granted. This was also after a lengthy argument before the judge about allowing Cashman to be called as a witness. The judge was considering the motion, but this District Attorney would go to any lengths to keep Cashman out of the courtroom.

The fifth notice of trial was in December 2021. This notice was served right after the continuance that the District Attorney asked for and received for the last notice of trial. This was reset due to the holidays.

The sixth notice of trial was in January 2022. This was reset by the judge to set the trial date in July 2022.

Every time a trial date was set, the defense attorneys had to put all other cases they had on hold and begin trial preparation. You just don't walk into a courtroom unprepared when a man's life depends on the outcome. No, you have to walk into that courtroom ready to fight for your client's life with every legal tool available. The defense attorneys had to do this six times since 2019, and it takes weeks if not months to prepare each time for a capital murder case. A defense team had better prepare and put on their game face when the stakes are this high—a man's life is on the line.

Chapter 15
Day 1 of Trial

That brings us to July 2022. The prosecution is on the left side of the courtroom next to the jury box, and the defense team is on the right side. The judge has given both sides notice that he wanted to have a jury seated on the first day.

Jury selection began right after lunch. The prosecution and defense quickly sifted through more than 250 juror questionnaires. This is the only chance to disqualify multiple jurors from the juror pool. After prospective jurors are released based on the juror questionnaire that each juror filled out, the remaining jurors were called in one at a time in a predetermined order and were then asked a series of questions from the prosecution team and the defense team. At this point in the juror selection process, the prosecution and the defense each have six juror strikes they can use to excuse a potential juror.

So, if you are not able to disqualify a juror based on questions answered on the questionnaire, then a jury will be selected within the next 26 jurors that are called up. Even if a potential juror has a conflict of interest, you may never know it because you only have six strikes. Under these guidelines, it seems to this writer that a jury could be easily manipulated by the District Attorney's office. The court clerk sends out the juror notices, and of course the court clerk works day in and day out in the same small courthouse as the District Attorney. It's a small rural community where everyone knows everyone else.

Anyway, at about 5:00 p.m., a jury was in place. Jury selection started around 1:00 p.m., and the judge made the attorneys select a jury in less than 4 hours. Did I mention that this was a capital murder case? This timeline to select a jury was unprecedented, to say the least. The trial would begin the next morning at 9:00 a.m. You could cut the tension in the air with a knife. Everyone was putting on a strong front, but so scared. How could we not be terrified? Michael's life was hanging in the balance. The tension was so thick that it was hard to even breathe. It's very painful to try to describe all the feelings at this point.

Chapter 16
Day 2 of The Trial

The prosecution began with their opening statement. There was a female Assistant District Attorney present who gave the opening statement.

Right out of the gate, the Assistant District Attorney stated that Michael discarded the mystery phone that was allegedly found submerged in a puddle of water in a roadside ditch on the interstate. This is clear and unmistakable misconduct, designed to purposely lie and mislead a jury. The Assistant District Attorney was fully aware that Michael's DNA had been excluded from the mystery phone and by none other than their own state crime lab. She said that after the incident, Michael went home and talked football with his dad, ate a banana, and went to sleep. All of those statements were meant to anger, alienate, and mislead the jury. One thing you can say, she has learned how to make up a story.

She did not stop there, though. She was on a roll. She continued by saying that Sapphire was the only person still alive that day who could say what happened. I guess she forgot about the defendant sitting not fifteen feet away from her, as well as the fourth person they never bothered to find. What an unethical, lying shrew.

Then, she stated that Jade was the leader of this organization. They had seen the same evidence and more on Cashman as has been listed in earlier chapters, but this Assistant DA was deliberately misleading the jury on the facts again.

Now it seems that she must tell some truths to get out in front of the real evidence. She did acknowledge that these women were not good people and ran their business across the United States and even around the world. At times the women involved in this business would make tens of thousands of dollars in just a couple of hours. They worked seven days a week, no days off, even having to turn away business. Wow! The Assistant District Attorney just called aggravated robbery, kidnapping, sex trafficking, threats to do bodily harm, and murder a business. Those poor overworked ruthless and vile criminals.

The Assistant District Attorney also went through the day before where Michael had replied to their ad on the internet. She stated that Michael got undressed and solicited Cinnamon and Sapphire for sex. Even Sapphire had rejected that statement and stated that never happened! It was just another incendiary statement, a misdirection, a lie.

She said that when the first officer on the scene asked Sapphire what happened, Sapphire stated that she had been on her phone and saw nothing until she heard the two gunshots. But didn't the Assistant District Attorney just say Sapphire was the only person alive that truly knew what happened that evening? She even admitted that they could not prove or disprove Michael's account of the events of that night.

This Assistant District Attorney couldn't help herself—she had to taunt Michael. So, she deliberately repeatedly referred to his daughter as "Cinnamon," the name of one of the girls who had threatened Michael and his entire family! She repeatedly used this method to try to provoke a response from him and to influence the jury against him.

The Assistant District Attorney faulted Michael for not giving a full statement on the early morning interview with the Texas Ranger. She stated that Michael should have been telling everyone that would listen about what had happened. Apparently, there is no right to remain silent. Just forget about that inconvenient part of the Constitution.

Chapter 17
The Defense Opening Statement

The defense attorney came out and discussed the events that led up to Michael's use of deadly force and described the events of that evening. He explained that Michael regularly went for a massage a few times a month, so when he saw a site on the Internet for an erotic massage, he made contact and soon after made an appointment. He explained that getting a massage is not against the law.

He continued and told the jury what happened to Michael that day, how Cinnamon and Sapphire had shown him that they had a gun and drove him to multiple banks in an attempt to drain all his bank accounts.

Then the defense attorney described the events of that evening. He described this as just a normal day with a happy family. He added that Michael was just happy to get away from Cinnamon and Sapphire alive and just wanted to continue his life and forget about what had happened that day.

Then he described to the jury that this organization would not stop – they were still coming after him. The defense attorney told the jury that they were the ones making the contact the second day, not Michael, and that Michael felt like he had no choice but to meet them again.

And then he described how Michael tried to give them another $2,100 and asked them to please leave him alone, but that Jade told him, "I am the girl today and the girl tomorrow and I will never stop coming."

He then told the jury that Jade told Michael to get out of the car because he was coming with them. Cinnamon opened his door and tugged at him and said, "If you fuck with us, you're dead."

He explained that that was when Michael noticed his gun was in the vehicle, so he pulled it and pointed it at Cinnamon and stated, "I am not getting back in that car."

Cinnamon then told him, "That's the last fucking mistake you're ever going to make" and reached for her bag. That was when Michael fired the first shot.

He then described to the jury that Michael then turned and looked at Jade and told her to give him his keys and cell phone and to just leave, but Jade kept moving towards him, reaching for the gun, so that's when he fired the second shot.

The defense attorney stated that what Michael did was not against the law, he was only defending himself, his property, and his family against multiple assailants. He was justified by the laws of Texas in the use of deadly force on that terrible night in November.

Chapter 18
Before the First Witness Is Called

At this time, the judge asked the District Attorney if he was still keeping the family under subpoena, to which he replied, "Absolutely."

So, Michael's family was directed to gather their belongings and get out of the courtroom and go to a conference room. The District Attorney had subpoenaed his entire family in a vicious and petty attempt to keep them out of the courtroom. After all, how would it look for the defendant to have people there to support him? He had told the judge that he intended on calling every one of the family members as witnesses; but of course, he never called any of the family as witnesses for the State – he just kept them isolated in that conference room for the entire trial.

Let's set the stage before the first witness takes the stand. The District Attorney had pretty much packed the courtroom with employees who work at the courthouse, law enforcement officials, and family and friends of the two women. There was even a county employee who was assigned the task of tending to the needs of the families of the women. Of course, Jade's mother did not arrive until week two because the District Attorney put the blame for all the organization's criminal activity onto Jade and stated that she was the leader and Cashman was not involved. There were also multiple people in the courtroom gallery every day from various advocacy groups from around town to show support for the women's families. Even the mother of one of the jurors was present with the prosecution side! Talk about playing to the audience. Unfortunately, this is a capital murder trial with a man's life on the line.

Chapter 19
The 911 Caller

The District Attorney is ready to call his first witness. The District Attorney rises and calls Mr. Martz to the stand. Mr. Martz came into the courtroom from the outside hallway, was sworn in, and took the stand.

District Attorney: What time was it was when you arrived at the bank?

Mr. Martz: It was around 6:45 p.m.

District Attorney: What did you observe happening at the bank that evening?

Mr. Martz: I saw Sapphire. She was leaning over the bodies, picking things up from them and around them on the ground. One of the items looked like a phone. She was very nervous. She said that her friends got into a fight and somebody shot them.

Mr. Martz also stated that the driver's door on the Mercedes was open when he arrived.

The District Attorney had no more questions, and the defense attorney asked no questions; so, Mr. Martz was allowed to leave. One thing that struck me most about the prosecutor calling this witness is that he did not call Mr. Martz's wife as a witness, and she was in the vehicle as well that evening.

Chapter 20
The First Officer on the Scene

The District Attorney called Officer Walters to the stand. Officer Walters entered the courtroom, was sworn in, and took the stand.

District Attorney: Officer Walters, were you working alone or with someone else that evening?

Officer Walters: I was alone.

District Attorney: Were any doors on the Mercedes open or were they all closed when you arrived?

Officer Walters: All the doors were closed.

District Attorney: When you arrived at the scene, where was Jade positioned?

Officer Walters: She was on the left side of the Mercedes sedan at the rear of the vehicle.

District Attorney: What did Sapphire tell you about what she witnessed?

Officer Walters: She stated that she looked up once after she heard the gunshots, and that's when she saw that they were dead.

The District Attorney had no further questions, nor did the defense attorney, so Officer Walters was excused.

Well Sapphire was at the rear of the Mercedes, same place Jade was lying; but now the door on the Mercedes is closed, whereas it was open when the

911 caller arrived. The 911 called did say Sapphire was picking up evidence. and she was where Jade was when the first officer arrived. The police and the Ranger never searched Sapphire for evidence she may have had on her person, they didn't search her car, they didn't even search her purse.

Sapphire desperately wanted the Ranger to let her go to the bathroom during the interview—maybe to dump evidence because she was afraid of being searched? There were a lot of police protocols skipped and ignored on that November evening. The question is why?

Chapter 21
The VP of the Bank

The District Attorney next called Mr. Kerr to the stand. Mr. Kerr entered the courtroom, was sworn in, and took the stand.

District Attorney: Mr. Kerr what is one of your duties at the bank?

Mr. Kerr: I manage the video surveillance.

District Attorney: Was there a camera on the east side of the bank on that date?

Mr. Kerr: No.

District Attorney: Can you describe the timeline of events that you observed for that evening?

Mr. Kerr: The defendant first arrived at the bank at 6:07 p.m. and parked. He pulled out and returned again and parked at 6:09 p.m. At 6:17 p.m., the defendant pulled out and parked in another spot. The defendant pulled out and drove around the bank. He came back and parked in the front of the bank. The defendant left at 6:27 p.m. and seemed to get stuck in a weird part of the parking lot. At 6:32 p.m. he pulled up to the ATM and parked, but did not attempt to use the ATM machine, and I observed him on his cell phone at that time.

At 6:33 p.m. the Honda pulled into the parking lot and parked, and the Mercedes arrived about a minute later at 6:34 p.m.

The next thing I observed was the Honda pulling out of the parking lot at 6:39:54 p.m. The red Hyundai pulled out at 6:40:30 p.m. or about 36 seconds later. At 6:44:40 p.m., I saw the 911 caller, Mr. Martz, pull up to the ATM. He used the ATM and then pulled forward like he was leaving, then stopped and got out of his vehicle.

The District Attorney had no further questions, and the defense attorney had no questions, so the witness was excused.

Chapter 22
The Hospital Police Officer

The District Attorney called Officer Steed to the stand. Officer Steed entered the courtroom, was sworn in, and took the stand.

District Attorney: Officer Steed, were you working at the hospital where the defendant worked on that day?

Officer Steed: I was on the 10:00 a.m. to midnight shift that day.

District Attorney: What does a normal shift look like?

Officer Steed: I work various complaints from employees and patrons and deal with assaults that happen every day.

District Attorney: Is there a check-in requirement to enter the department where the defendant worked?

Officer Steed: There is no requirement unless you're attempting to enter a locked patient core area.

District Attorney: Can you tell the jury what you observed when you viewed hospital video footage?

Officer Steed: I observed the defendant walking to the parking lot at 2:43:40 and returning to the building at 2:44:44 with two females, about 1 minute later. I then observed the defendant and the two females walking back to the parking lot at 2:54:58, or about 10 minutes later.

District Attorney: Have you ever observed or had reports of the defendant being angry or violent or try to pick a fight?

Officer Steed: I never have observed the defendant angry or violent, he was always pleasant and professional.

The District Attorney had no further questions, the defense attorney had no questions, so the witness was allowed to leave.

Chapter 23
The CSI Analyst

The District Attorney called Ms. Mann to the stand. Ms. Mann entered the courtroom, was sworn in, and took the stand.

District Attorney: Ms. Mann what was you occupation on that night?

Ms. Mann: I worked as the CSI analyst, although I was not certified or licensed at the time.

District Attorney: Who did you first talk to when you arrived at the incident scene?

Ms. Mann: Sgt. Smith.

District Attorney: What duties did you perform? Please describe them for the jury.

Ms. Mann: I took all the crime scene photos. The evidence cones were already placed when I arrived, so all I had to do was photograph the evidence. I usually do a walkthrough of the scene, but I did not need to do it this time. The bodies were already covered at this time. I don't know who covered them. Jade was lying at the back of the Mercedes sedan.

District Attorney: Anything else that you noticed or collected?

Ms. Mann: I saw a box of pop-its, unexpended. I didn't see any expended pop-its. There was an empty purse/bag in the back seat of the Honda and another purse/bag beside Cinnamon, both Louis Vuitton bags.

District Attorney: Did you tag and check evidence into the property room at the police department?

Ms. Mann: No. I turned it over to Sgt. Smith. She was responsible for items taken from the scene.

District Attorney: Did you interview the witness?

Ms. Mann: No, but I was aware that the Texas Ranger was speaking with her.

District Attorney: Where did you go after you left the scene?

Ms. Mann: A lot of us gathered at the Sheriff's office for a briefing at about 1:00 a.m., after getting something to eat. Then I went with the team and was part of serving the warrant and the search of the home.

District Attorney: What did you do at the defendant's parents' home?

Ms. Mann: I photographed every room and searched the entire house.

District Attorney: How did you know what room the defendant lived in?

Ms. Mann: I do not remember.

The defense attorney then questioned the witness.

Defense Attorney: Ms. Mann, who was in charge of this investigation at the bank?

Ms. Mann: It's hard to say, I can't say it was just one person. It was unclear who was in charge.

Defense Attorney: So, everyone just milled around doing their own thing without any direction or scene supervision.

Ms. Mann: I guess, you could say that.

Defense Attorney: Did you find computers in the trunk of the Mercedes sedan?

Ms. Mann: Yes, I saw seven brand new laptop computers, just purchased the day of the incident, and the receipt was there as well, totaling $7,202.78.

Defense Attorney: Let's talk about the night the defendant drove his vehicle through a car wash. If it was an attempt to clean off evidence, wouldn't you agree that it would have been a careless attempt?

Ms. Mann: Yes, if that was his intent, it was careless.

Defense Attorney: But you don't think that was his intention to clean off evidence?

Ms. Mann: I don't think it was, but I can't really say with any certainty.

Defense Attorney: Did you recover a gun at the scene?

Ms. Mann: No.

Defense Attorney: Did you search the two bags you found?

Ms. Mann: It's not in the report that I searched them, but I think I did... It's usually protocol.

Defense Attorney: So, you don't know if you searched the two bags, but you know there is not a report on what could have been in those two bags.

Ms. Mann: Correct.

Defense Attorney: So, if a gun was in one of those bags, there is no report on that.

Ms. Mann: I did not see a gun at the scene of the incident or take a photo of a gun.

The defense attorney had no further questions, nor did the District Attorney, so the witness was released.

Chapter 24
Day 3 of the Trial
The Texas Ranger

The District Attorney called the Texas Ranger to the stand. The Texas Ranger entered the courtroom, was sworn in, and took the stand.

District Attorney: Describe your duties as a Texas Ranger in this County.

Texas Ranger: I work with homicides and questionable deaths, and I have statewide jurisdiction.

District Attorney: Tell us about the scene of the incident and what you observed and did.

Texas Ranger: I saw two dead bodies in the parking lot. I met with Sgt. Smith and Ms. Mann and the Chief of Police. They told me there was a witness in the back of a patrol vehicle. I had the witness transferred to my vehicle, where I conducted an interview.

District Attorney: Tell us about that interview.

Texas Ranger: She was initially untruthful but eventually told me what I needed to know after interviewing her for three hours.

District Attorney: Were you concerned that Sapphire could have been the potential shooter?"

Texas Ranger: I had no reason to believe she was a potential shooter.

District Attorney: Was she being truthful with you during the interview?

Texas Ranger: She was not being truthful, and that's when I obtained her phone, took it.

District Attorney: Did you interview the defendant?

Texas Ranger: Yes, he was visibly upset, crying, sniffling, and scared.

District Attorney: What did the defendant tell you?

Texas Ranger: The defendant only stated that the women were going to traffic his daughter and that he should have told his wife and then did not say anything else.

District Attorney: After interviewing the defendant for about 20 minutes, what did you do next?

Texas Ranger: I booked two pistols taken from the home (neither related to the incident) and some clothes recovered from the home into evidence and went home.

District Attorney: Can you tell me about the Defendant's vehicle and what happened to it?

Texas Ranger: I know it was transported to one location and then a couple of days later transported to a local car dealerships body shop. The vehicle sat at the body shop in a public parking lot until evidence was collected and the vehicle searched and then later was transported to another location. Most of the evidence was kept by Sgt. Smith.

District Attorney: Did the defendant ever say where he put his gun that night?

Texas Ranger: Yes, I received instruction that the defendant notified your office about a week after the incident about where to find the gun used at the scene. About a month later, we took the defendant on a field trip to locate the weapon.

District Attorney: Did you locate the gun?

Texas Ranger: No, we did not.

District Attorney: Did you continue to search for the weapon or ask workers in the area if they found a gun?

Texas Ranger: No, I did not.

District Attorney: How was Sapphire acting during the interview you did with her?

Texas Ranger: Sapphire was very calm.

District Attorney: Judge I would like to take a lunch break now; and when we return, I would like to call the Medical Examiner to the stand and then re-call the Texas Ranger later.

Judge: Any objections, defense?

Defense? No objections your honor.

Judge: Let's break for lunch. Be back at 1:00 p.m.

Chapter 25
The Medical Examiner

The District Attorney called the medical examiner to the stand. The medical examiner entered the courtroom, was sworn in, and took the stand.

District Attorney: Can you describe the cause of death and injuries on Jade?

Medical Examiner: Gunshot wound on the right side of the chin; cause of death was a gunshot wound. Other injuries were consistent with falling. I estimated that she was shot from two to four feet away. Jade landed on her left side. Toxicology showed positive THC in her blood.

District Attorney: How about Cinnamon?

Medical Examiner: Similar wounds, fractured pelvic bone. X-rays showed skull fracture, fragments of the bullet in the head, pelvic fracture consistent with being run over. Gunshot wound to left forehead (temple), exited back of head, some fragments that were left behind, and a black eye from blood pooling. Toxicology showed positive, she had THC in her blood.

The District Attorney had no further questions, the defense attorney had no questions, so the witness was released.

Chapter 26
The Ranger Returns

The District Attorney again called the Texas Ranger to the stand. The Texas Ranger entered the courtroom, was reminded that he was still under oath, and took the stand.

District Attorney: What evidence did you handle as part of this incident?

Texas Ranger: Cars, large interviews, crime labs, back and forth to the house and the bank the morning of the search, and the field trip with the defendant to attempt to locate the gun used in the shooting.

The District Attorney had no further questions, so the defense attorney questioned the witness.

Defense Attorney: Ranger who was in charge of the investigation?

Texas Ranger: I do not know.

Defense Attorney: What was Sgt. Smith's role in this investigation?

Texas Ranger: Taking direction from other officers.

Defense Attorney: What was Ms. Mann's role in this investigation?

Texas Ranger: Taking direction from other officers, same as Sgt. Smith.

Defense Attorney: Didn't Sapphire tell you she was not afraid of Michael because she stated, "He had every chance to shoot me, but he didn't"?

Texas Ranger: Yes.

Defense Attorney: Did you not consider the crimes this organization had committed and were committing?

Texas Ranger: I didn't give a dam what they did, and I still don't.

Defense Attorney – (Shows a picture of the vehicles the four people arrived at the bank in.) Are these the vehicles they were driving?

Texas Ranger: I am not for sure if that's the vehicles or which one is which.

Defense Attorney: The Texas Penal code states that deadly force is permitted for robbery or threats or when someone places another in fear of imminent bodily injury or death. Is that true?

Texas Ranger: Yes.

Defense Attorney: Cinnamon had a jacket. What happened to it?

Texas Ranger: We searched for it but never found it. We searched the perimeter but did not find it.

Defense Attorney: Did you search the gas station across the street.

Texas Ranger: No.

Defense Attorney: Knowing what you know now about the crimes these women had and were committing, including Sapphire, do you regret not charging her with the she was committing?

Texas Ranger: I don't regret letting her go.

Defense Attorney: Why did you not investigate Cashman for sex trafficking and all the other crimes his organization was committing?

Texas Ranger – The police department recently referred him a few months ago to the FBI for suspected sex trafficking.

The defense attorney had no further questions for the Ranger, nor did the prosecution, so he was released.

Well, the Ranger's testimony sure raises more questions than answers about how they were protecting the organized crime group. They knew the crimes being committed, they referred Cashman to the FBI for possible sex trafficking, so why is Michael still on trial for a capital murder charge?

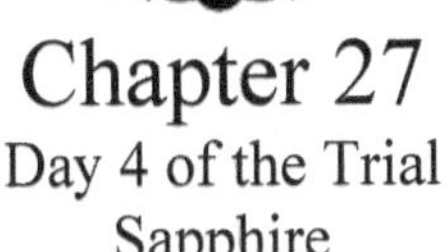

Chapter 27
Day 4 of the Trial
Sapphire

Okay, let's keep this to changes in this witness's story since we have all read her witness statement the night of the incident.

The District Attorney called Sapphire to the stand. Sapphire entered the courtroom, was sworn in, and took the stand.

District Attorney: Sapphire what is your current employment?

Sapphire: I clean houses. (Bet she cleans them out real good, too).

District Attorney: How old are you?

Sapphire: Then 23, now 28.

District Attorney: What was life like growing up?

Sapphire: Abused in high school and left home at age 14. I made a hit list of students, teachers, and parents I wanted to kill, and they kicked me out of school.

District Attorney: Do you have any kids?

Sapphire: Yes, but I have had no contact with them since they were 8 months old. They live with their father.

District Attorney: Are you from this area?"

Sapphire: No, Jade recruited me from the Texas Panhandle. And, besides, I have known Cashman for a long time. I assumed Jade was a stripper. Jade made the trip to the Panhandle to pick me up.

District Attorney: Anyone else living with you and Jade?

Sapphire: Yes. Cinnamon and Cashman and Annie. I was closest with Cinnamon.

District Attorney: Who owned the house you were living in?

Sapphire: Cashman.

District Attorney – "What was it like when you got there?"

Sapphire: There were two Mercedes in the driveway, Cashman paid for everything, we traveled all over the place doing our business every day. We stayed at one hotel where the elevator went to our suite and the suite was the whole floor. We got stacks of cash every day. Jade got a Rolex. We were all getting luxury items. We even got a cash machine counter to count all the cash our business was bringing in.

District Attorney: How did Cinnamon come to be there?

Sapphire: She came straight from rehab to be there, not for sure of how or why.

District Attorney: Is there anything else that happened?

Sapphire?   Cashman got us social security cards and driver's licenses for ID's.

District Attorney: How many calls did you answer a day?

Sapphire: I went to 20 or more a day. We had plenty of business. I went everywhere.

District Attorney: Have you worked in this county before this incident?

Sapphire: Oh, yeah, many times.

District Attorney: What drugs did you and the others use?

Sapphire: Mainly marijuana and cocaine.

District Attorney: What about clothes and shoes? Did you buy them?

Sapphire: Yes, and we got to keep the clothes and shoes, but all the jewelry went to Jade and Cashman.

District Attorney: What did Jade tell you about the business with the defendant that day?

Sapphire: She was excited. She texted us, "We're going shopping." We ran into another guy at Wal-Mart that same night and bought a bunch of computers, $7,202.78 worth, and got a $100.00 cash back on his card. We had told him we would take his dog if he didn't pay us. After that, Jade decided that we were going to hit Michael again.

District Attorney: What did the defendant do when you all pulled in and parked.

Sapphire: He pulled up behind our cars and put his hand out the window. I couldn't see what was in his hand. Jade tried to get in his vehicle, but his doors were locked. Jade told him to pull into a parking place and park and pointed to the parking spot. Then Jade got into the passenger front seat and Cinnamon got into the driver side rear seat.

District Attorney: What did you lie about the night of the incident?

Sapphire: I lied about a lot of stuff. I lied about giving the defendant a massage, I left a lot of things out.

At this point, the District Attorney had no more questions. The defense attorney then questioned the witness.

Defense Attorney: How many calls have you done with your so-called business, you know, your criminal activity?

Sapphire: A lot, 20-30 a day. I have done hundreds.

Defense Attorney: People will just give you $7,000 or more, no problem, even if they are terrified?

Sapphire: Yes, no problem, we always get the money and property.

Defense Attorney: Whose house were you all living in?

Sapphire: Cashman's.

Defense Attorney: Whose cars were all you are driving?

Sapphire: Cashman's. He had just bought them for us to drive.

Defense Attorney: Who was the aggressor?

Sapphire: Cinnamon was the aggressive one, and I was the calmer one. We were trained not to stop. We would use threats and say ***whatever we needed*** to say or do to get whatever we needed or wanted to get.

At this time the defense attorney finished questioning, and the witness was released. No better place to stop day four than with the District Attorney, law enforcement, and the court protecting this organized crime group. They just let Sapphire walk away, knowing full well that she had just admitted to committing thousands of felony crimes. But who is protecting their victims?

Chapter 28
Day 5 of the Trial
Sgt. Smith

District Attorney called Sgt. Smith to the stand. Sgt. Smith entered the courtroom, was sworn in, and took the stand.

District Attorney: Were you on duty on that night?

Sgt. Smith: No, I was called in.

District Attorney: Who was first on the scene?

Sgt. Smith: I do not know.

District Attorney: Had you ever worked a shooting or a homicide before?

Sgt. Smith: No.

District Attorney: Did you interview the witness or the 911 caller?

Sgt. Smith: No.

District Attorney: What was your position with the police department in November 2017?

Sgt. Smith: I oversaw the property room.

The District Attorney had no more questions for the witness, so the defense attorney questioned the witness.

Defense Attorney: Were you at the home when it was searched?

Sgt. Smith: No.

Defense Attorney: Were you there when the defendant was arrested?

Sgt. Smith: No.

Defense Attorney: (Showed Sgt. Smith pictures of the mystery phone found in puddle of water) Was the phone still on when it was pulled out of the puddle of water?

Sgt. Smith: Yes.

Defense Attorney: Did you know they robbed the defendant and took $8,000?

Sgt. Smith: No.

Defense Attorney: Did you know they robbed the defendant for another $2,100 and threatened him and his family and to traffic his daughter the night of the incident?

Sgt. Smith: No.

Defense Attorney: Did you know these women would pose as massage therapists?

Sgt. Smith: No.

Defense Attorney: Did detectives from Dallas County send you a report on this organization and that these women were involved in similar incident where they used guns?

Sgt. Smith: I don't remember seeing it or reviewing it.

Defense Attorney: Here's a copy of the report. Does that refresh your memory?

Smith: No.

The defense attorney said he had no more questions at that time but wished to retain the witness for the future. The judge called for a break.

Following the break, the District Attorney re-called Sgt. Smith.

District Attorney: During the break, did you have time to review the report from Dallas County?

Sgt. Smith: Yes, and none of the details were ever validated by the detectives involved, and they never proved that they used guns. The person that filed the complaint left town and stopped cooperating with the police, and they could not find him anymore.

The prosecution had no further questions for Sgt. Smith, and the witness was released.

Funny how Sgt. Smith could recall all those details after meeting with the prosecutors during the break. You know the old saying—if it looks like a duck and quacks like a duck and walks like a duck then it's most likely a duck. Does Sgt. Smith look and sound like a liar?

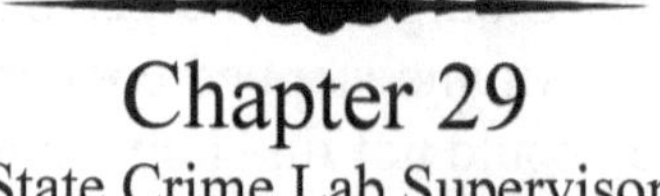

Chapter 29
State Crime Lab Supervisor

The District Attorney called the State Crime Lab supervisor to testify. The State Crime Lab Supervisor entered the courtroom, was sworn in, and took the stand.

District Attorney: Tell us about the tests you performed on the phone that was found on the side of the interstate several days following the incident.

State Crime Lab Supervisor: We performed extensive DNA swab tests of the phone; and although there was a mixture of multiple DNA from multiple persons on the phone that we could not identify, Michael and Jade both were excluded as having come in contact with the phone.

The District Attorney had no further questions, so the defense attorney questioned the witness.

Defense Attorney: Was a DNA sample tested from Sapphire?

State Crime Lab Supervisor: No.

Defense Attorney: Was a sample of Cashman's DNA submitted for testing?

State Crime Lab Supervisor: No, it was not.

Defense Attorney: And Michael's DNA was definitely not found on that phone?

State Crime Lab Supervisor? That is correct.

The defense attorney had no further questions, and the witness was released.

The Prosecution Rests Their Case

Well, it appears that the District Attorney spent five days proving that Michael shot Cinnamon and Jade. Congratulations and surprise! We all already knew that Michael shot Cinnamon, and Jade and he has claimed self-defense. So, why did the District Attorney bring so many witnesses to prove that Michael pulled the trigger? That's not as big a mystery as it may seem to be. The District Attorney already stated to the jury that he could not prove or disprove Michael's account of events the night of the incident. Obviously, all he can do is attempt to confuse and manipulate and mislead the jurors.

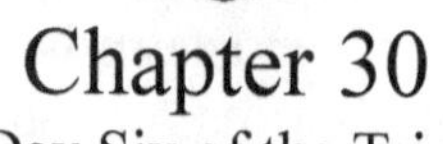

Chapter 30
Day Six of the Trial
Another Victim

The defense attorney called their first witness to the stand. Stan entered the courtroom, was sworn in, and took the stand.

Defense Attorney: Tell us what happened when you encountered this group."

The District Attorney at this time objected 10 times in a row to this witness. However, the judge over-ruled his objections.

Defense Attorney: Again, please tell us about your experience with this group.

Stan: I responded to a Backpage ad. Two women showed up instead of one, and I did not want to let them in, but they said, "More fun with 2." I still did not want to let them in.

The District Attorney again objected and again was over-ruled.

Stan: They pushed their way in, and they were very aggressive. Cinnamon started walking through the apartment, going through all my papers and closets.

The District Attorney continued to object as to "hearsay" but was again over-ruled by the Judge.

Stan: Cinnamon told me she would tell my wife I was soliciting minors.

District Attorney objected again and the judge over-ruled the objection.

Stan: I asked them to leave. They began tossing stuff around the apartment and threatening me. They went through my son's closet said they would wait outside his school for him. They continued to threaten me and emasculate me. It was the worst trauma in my life. I was very scared. I was helpless. I went for my phone to call the police They said, "Don't do that, or I'll call my man in that's waiting outside the door and you'll get pistol whipped at best." I felt utterly helpless against them. They took my wife's cell phone and they put it in a big bag they carried on their shoulder. They took everything and left.

Defense: Did you report it to the police?

Stan: No, they said if I called the police they would go for my kid at his school.

The defense had no further questions, so the District Attorney questioned the witness.

District Attorney: So, they started beating you up over calling prostitutes.

Stan: "I don't know why they were beating and robbing me.

District Attorney: What did you tell your wife?

Stan: I told her we got robbed.

District Attorney: Why did you not pull a gun on them?

Stan: I don't own a gun.

District Attorney: Why did you not call the police?

Stan: They threatened to go to my kid's school.

District Attorney: Did you see a gun?

Stan: I believed them when they told me they had
a gun. They were trained and very good at what they
were doing. They were experts.

The District Attorney had no more questions, and
the defense attorney had no more questions, so the
witness was excused.

Chapter 31
The Defendant's Mother

The Defense called Michael's mother to the stand. She was understandably scared and nervous. The defense started by asking what Michael's demeaner was like, and here is where a mother's love shines. She explained that Michael is very sensitive and soft and sweet. Moms have a special way of describing their children like no one else can.

The defense asked her if Michael is a violent person, and she replied, "No, I have never seen him in a rage, and I have never seen him get in a fight. He always tries to calm people and de-escalate any tension."

The Assistant District Attorney stepped up and asked what Michael did when he came home. His mom stated he walked slowly through the kitchen, looked around, then went upstairs for a shower. Later, he came down and took a couple of bites of a banana and then went back upstairs. She stated she did not see him again that night. The witness was retained by the District Attorney after she testified so that she could not be in the courtroom to support her son.

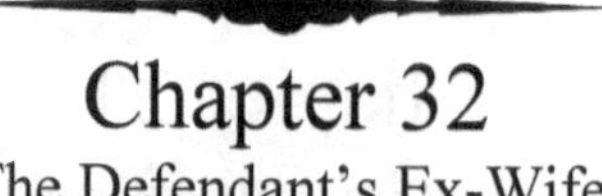

Chapter 32
The Defendant's Ex-Wife

The defense attorney asked the ex-wife, Lacy, when she and Michael got divorced. She stated about a year ago. She also stated that even though both of them had affairs during the marriage, there were more good times than bad. The defense attorney asked about Michael's demeaner.

She said, "He's goofball, he always kidding and joking around. He just wants to make everyone happy. Michael is a very calm man. Even when I tried to make him mad, I couldn't. He just would not fight or argue with me."

The defense attorney asked, "Do you have a daughter."

She replied, "Yes, she was 14 at the time. Michael had adopted her, and you would never know he was not her birth father. He loves her with all his heart and would do anything to protect her."

Then, the Assistant District Attorney stepped up and asked, "Did the defendant tell anyone about what went on the day before or the day of the incident?"

Lacy stated, "Not that I am aware of. He wanted to protect us all, not panic us all."

The Assistant District Attorney asked, "Did you know he was soliciting prostitutes."

To which Lacy responded, "To my knowledge he hired someone for a massage, not a prostitute."

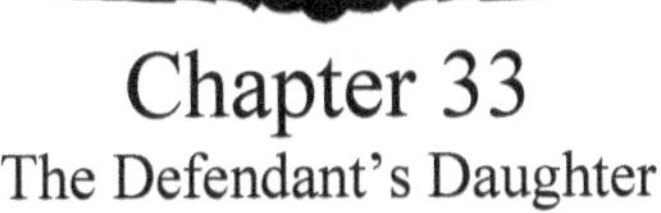

Chapter 33
The Defendant's Daughter

The defense attorney then called Michael's daughter to the stand and asked what her dad means to her. With tears running down her face, she looked at her dad at the defense table. Michael was crying as well.

She stated, "He is my best friend, he is everything to me. I don't know what I would do without him. He saved me from my child predator birth dad."

She and Michael were both openly crying at this point. The Assistant District Attorney wasn't satisfied with that, though. She berated the daughter, stating that her father was a sex predator as well, and she continued rapid firing questions at her, not even allowing her time to answer, just yelling questions at her. It was an obvious attempt to provoke a reaction from Michael. The judge finally had to step in and stop the Assistant District Attorney, stating "That's enough, one question at a time," but by this time Michael's daughter was crying uncontrollably and in a full-on panic attack. The Assistant District Attorney stated she had no more questions and turned and smiled at Michael and said she was retaining the witness.

The daughter returned to the small conference room where she continued to have a panic attack and having trouble breathing. This turned into a medical emergency. as Michael's daughter is about six months pregnant. Michael's father asked the deputy at the front desk to call for an ambulance. Paramedics came in and evaluated her and wanted to take her to the hospital. But at that point, about an hour after the vicious attack by the Assistant District Attorney, there was a court break and Michael was able to come into the room. He was able to calm her down. As I said, Michael is really good at helping people in distress. She finally stabilized, and the judge allowed her to go home for the rest of the day.

During the break, the district attorney was by the jury room with jurors going in and out, and he was brazenly discussing the case in front of the jurors. When this conduct was mentioned in court, before he knew he was busted, that District Attorney actually attempted to blame Michael's family for juror tampering (from the conference room?!). The Judge quickly cut him off quickly and stated, "We will discuss this in chambers." Of course, the judge said nothing to Michael's family. He recognized the situation.

Of course, that didn't solve everything. Another problem kept occurring during the trial as well—a juror kept falling asleep during testimony. The judge finally moved that juror close to the bailiff so they could try to keep her awake.

Chapter 34
The Use of Force Expert

The use of force expert began reading off his credentials and experience—Director of a firearms specialist academy, raising the bar on firearms training with multiple day seminars and training, retired ATF agent, criminal investigator with the ATF related to deadly weapons.

The District Attorney asked if he had been in court during the state's case the week before, and he stated, "No."

He explained that the distance between multiple assailants can increase the risk/danger. The District Attorney objected to this witness but was overrule and the witness was allowed to testify. The use of force expert testified on the what the Texas penal code stated was justification in self-defense using deadly force and stated that it included, protecting one's own property, robbery, aggravated robbery, defense of self and or others, if you felt your life was in imminent danger, forcible entry into your home or vehicle, kidnapping or aggravated kidnapping, multiple assailants, etc. The use of force expert stated that Michael had multiple reasons under the Texas self-defense statutes to use deadly force on that evening in 2017, or even the day before. *The prosecution offered no expert in rebuttal to this defense expert's opinions and conclusions*

Chapter 35
Voir Dire of the Experts

Voir Dire of the Forensics Expert for the Defense

The defense called the forensics ballistics expert to the stand; and when he began to detail his experience, the District Attorney stood up and stated that they would not be contesting this witness's qualifications but that he did want to cross-examine on matters of testimony. The District Attorney asked him what reports he reviewed to prepare for his testimony, and the expert replied that he had reviewed the Texas Ranger's report, Sgt. Smith's report, the CSI report, other officer reports, autopsy reports, CSI photos, home photos, car photos, the clothing, and crime lab photos.

Voir Dire of the FBI/Trafficking Expert

The District Attorney fought hard to keep this expert off the stand because he would be testifying on pimp-prostitute relationships and human trafficking. The District Attorney knew that this expert's testimony directly points to the Crime Boss, Cashman. The defense attorney called Daniel, and he began to state his qualifications and experience. He is a federal agent with Homeland Security, on the Human Trafficking Task Force, and has worked undercover both nationally and internationally. Daniel continued to state that he has reviewed phone dumps, reports, videos, and interviews. He described Jade as the person who maintains the "stable." She would be known as the "bottom bitch" or "#1 girl" and would maintain stability with all the other women. Sapphire was not at the same level as all the other women. She still depended on the pimp for everything. Daniel also stated that emails to Cinnamon from Cashman showed that Cashman had to give permission for the women to do something as simple as getting their nails done. He stated that they ran a different scheme than prostitution but it's the same hierarchy within Cashman's organization. The District Attorney asked what was the relevance to this case, and Daniel stated he would show the control Cashman had and what Jade's position was and that the women would have done or said anything to get money for Cashman or to protect him. And in this case, the bottom bitch/#1 girl was sent to finish the job.

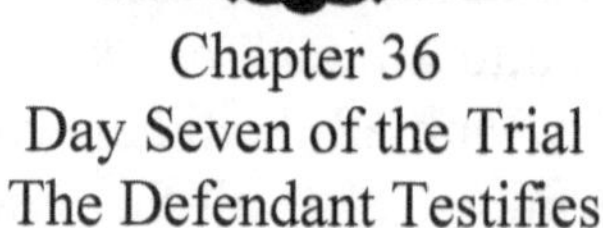

Chapter 36
Day Seven of the Trial
The Defendant Testifies

The Defense called Michael to the stand, and he stated that yes, he reached out to the advertisement for a massage. (Sapphire had also confirmed many times that the advertisement was for a massage, not prostitutes). The District Attorney would have none of that because it just did not fit the narrative of the fairy tale he was spinning; so he continued to say that Michael hired prostitutes, even though he knew full well that was not the case and that he was misleading the jury.

Michael continued to talk about what happened when Cinnamon and Sapphire showed up at the scheduled time for a massage. He also stated that he never touched them in any way. They told him to prepare for the massage and get undressed, and that's what he did—he stripped down to his underwear. If you have ever been to a professional spa, then you know you strip down completely for a massage. Michael then stated that they began to go through his desk and his clothes pockets and his wallet. He said the women threatened to scream rape if he did anything to try to stop them. Then, he said, Cinnamon displayed a gun and told him he was coming with them. Cinnamon and Sapphire, as we now know, were not massage therapists, and they were not

140

prostitutes, they were hardened and well-trained criminals. They had been well trained in how to commit aggravated robbery, theft, aggravated kidnapping, and terroristic threats to kill and/or traffic family members. As Sapphire stated, they were trained to do whatever it took to get what they needed, never stop. These facts of the case are indisputable at this point in the trial, and the District Attorney knows that and has admitted it, but he continues to lie and mislead the jury. These criminal acts were Cashman's organized crime group's daily routine that they had perfected on 50 plus victims per day, seven days a week.

Michael stated he went with Cinnamon and Sapphire because there were a lot of patients and employees everywhere and he was worried about everyone's safety. At this point Cinnamon had already displayed a gun to him. So, he went quietly, terrified. He stated that Cinnamon and Sapphire brought him around to multiple banks and attempted to drain every penny they could. Then, they drove him around a while and dumped him out on the street.

The District Attorney said if it were not for men and women like Michael hiring prostitutes, these businesses would not exist. Again, Michael had hired them for a massage. He did not respond to a prostitution advertisement, and those women were not prostitutes.

Michael admitted shooting Jade and Cinnamon the following evening and explained that he did it in self-defense. Michael tearfully, sobbing uncontrollably at times, stated that he never wanted to hurt anyone, never meant to kill anyone, but they left him no choice—he was not going to get into their vehicle late on a Saturday night or at any other time again, and he was not going to allow them to traffic his 14-year-old daughter. They knew they already had all his money, and there were no banks open at that time of night. The District Attorney admitted that he could not prove or disprove the events that Michael described, and he could not disprove that Michael acted in self-defense. And because we know the evidence at this point, we know the truth. We know that his action was based on self-defense and permitted by the laws in Texas.

Michael explained that he was terrified and in shock after the shooting, and he admitted he made some mistakes in judgement, like leaving the scene, not calling 911, hiding the gun, and not telling anyone. None of us know how we would act or what we would do in the same situation as Michael that night, and with the grace of God I hope you are never in that situation and will never experience the terror that he faced in that bank parking lot on that fall evening.

Chapter 37
The Forensics Expert

The forensics expert presented a 3-D video recreation of the scene to the jury and testified to the jury about the trajectory of the shots. Cinnamon was shot in the left side of the head in the temple area. If she was facing Michael, why was she not hit the front portion of the head? If she was running away, why was she not hit in the back of the head? The expert testified that Cinnamon was facing Michael at the time of the shooting, but as Michael had described, Cinnamon was reaching into a large bag on her right shoulder, the bag that she pulled a gun out of the day before. This action meant that she had turned slightly, resulting in the gunshot hitting her in the side of the head and not the front of her head. Cinnamon then fell to her right side. The expert explained that when someone is shot and either is killed instantly or blacks out instantly, the person will fall in the direction they were traveling at the time. The expert stated that Cinnamon was turning to her right when struck by the bullet that killed her instantly, and so she fell to the right, face down.

The expert then explained that Jade was struck in the lower right side of her chin with the bullet traveling in an upward path and through the back of the head. Jade was positioned between the right side of Michael's vehicle and the left side of her vehicle, with the bank directly behind her. The expert continued to say that Jade had exited Michael's vehicle from the right front passenger door and at this point Michael was positioned at the right rear of his vehicle. The expert explained that Michael had stated that Jade was moving towards him and reaching for the gun and that he could confirm that statement with the evidence. If Jade had been shot while getting out of either vehicle, the bullet would have travelled in a downward trajectory and exited out her neck or back, but that is not the case here. The bullet entered the right side of her chin in an upward trajectory, instantly causing her death.

The expert continued to explain that as Jade moved towards Michael, reaching for his weapon with her right hand, reaching out and extending her right arm and hand, her body was twisting to the left slightly. Jade fell onto her left side after being shot, and this was confirmed in the medical examiner's report as well. Jade fell to her left side because that was the direction, her body was traveling when shot and killed. The expert testified that Jade was shot from 3 to 4 inches away from the gun. Her position after being shot was lying on her left side with her right arm extended in front of her body and her left arm down to her side, again confirming that she was reaching towards Michael at the time she was shot.

The District Attorney had another forensics ballistics expert watching in the courtroom, listening to the defense expert's explanations of the crime scene. His conclusions confirmed the statements made by the defense witness about the events. The defense expert's conclusions of the evidence were sound and indisputable. With that conclusion, the District Attorney released their own expert and did not offer a rebuttal to the defense expert's conclusions.

145

Chapter 38
The FBI/Trafficking Expert

The defense called the trafficking expert. This expert has never testified or worked with any defense team in any trial in the past. He worked with Homeland Security investigations on domestic and international human trafficking and smuggling cases. This witness was instrumental in explaining the hierarchy within Cashman's organized crime group, especially, since the District Attorney was telling the jury that Cashman had nothing to do with what the women were doing. The trafficking expert reviewed all the phone information, pictures, and texts between the group and stated that the women in this organization would do or say anything for or to protect Cashman.

The expert went on to describe how Cashman used and empowered his bottom bitch or #1 girl. The #1 girl in this case was Jade. She was in charge of keeping the women in line and working every day of the week. The expert stated that he reviewed emails from the women to Cashman where they had to ask for his permission to do or buy anything and had to tell Cashman any time they left and where they were going.

He also explained the reason for Cashman's plea deal and charges from his 2010 conviction. He stated that the feds do not investigate prostitution, and so they charged him with interstate money laundering. The expert testified that he had reviewed Stan's testimony that the women threatened that they had a man in the hallway had a gun, ready to come in, as well as the Dallas County report where the women used guns on a victim in that case; and he testified that he had no reason to believe that they did not have a gun with then in this case.

The expert stated that he read a text from Cinnamon to Jade saying, "Hey, why don't we traffic the young girl. That would be fun." He stated that the women had to do everything they could to get what they needed to get for Cashman and that Michael had good reason to be terrified and scared for his life and the life of his family.

The District Attorney did not call a rebuttal expert to refute any of the facts, opinions, and/or conclusions of this expert witness. But in closing arguments, he used a racially demeaning nickname that he made up for this witness to bias the jury against him.

Chapter 39
Day 8 of The Trial
Closing Statements

The night before closing statements, Michael went out for dinner with his mom, dad, and little brother. After a quiet dinner at a local restaurant, the family and Michael took a moment to talk in the parking lot. Michael had been trying so hard to be strong for his family throughout the trial, but the wall came crashing down and Michael broke down crying in his father's arms, saying "I am so scared."

His father just held him for about 15 minutes and tried to reassure him that God would see him through all the lies and intentional false and misleading statements by the prosecution.

His father reminded him of "Psalm 23: The LORD *is* my shepherd; I shall not want. He maketh me to lie down in green pastures: he leadeth me beside the still waters. He restoreth my soul: He leadeth me in the paths of righteousness for his name's sake. Yea, though I walk through the valley of the shadow of death, I will fear no evil: for thou art with me; thy rod and thy staff they comfort me. Thou preparest a table before me in the presence of my enemies: thou anoint my head with oil; my cup runneth over. Surely goodness and mercy shall follow

148

me all the days of my life: and I will dwell in the house of the LORD forever."

Michael's mom, dad, and little brother continued to comfort Michael until he was able to regain composure and was able to drive home. But all that comfort could not mask the fear that shook him to his core, the fact that his life would soon be in the hands of 12 strangers. "What are they thinking? Do they believe the fairy tales that the prosecution is spinning? Do they see that the District Attorney has offered no evidence at all that I was not justified in using deadly force? Do they see the truth about the events that horrible evening in November?" Michael will be forever scared by what has happened, and his family will as well, but will he receive justice from the small-town rural jury, or will this unethical District Attorney get the verdict he craves and continue the victimization of this innocent family man. We are approaching the verdict quickly now.

The District Attorney's First Closing Arguments

The Assistant District Attorney started off, with no surprise, stating that Michael took Jade's phone and tossed it out the window on his way home and then did not go to the police and did not call 911 but did dump the gun and did go wash his car. The Assistant District Attorney stated that that evening Michael went to meet Jade, Cinnamon, and Sapphire and then killed them, but she did not offer an explanation or refer to any evidence as to why he shot them, just that he shot them. The Assistant District Attorney, of course, failed to reference the 4th person. She stated that Michael got out of the vehicle and "just executed those girls," shooting Cinnamon first and then walking around the vehicle and shooting Jade. The Assistant District Attorney failed to offer a reason why Michael shot Cinnamon and Jade. She spent the rest of her closing time talking about the women being from broken homes, running away at an early age, their drug abuse, and how they were not on drugs now. She must have been asleep during Sapphire's testimony when she admitted that they all used marijuana and cocaine regularly. This District Attorney's office goes by their own laws and will do anything to win. The judge informed the Assistant District Attorney that her time was up.

The Defense Closing Argument

This will be quick. You have all read the evidence and know Michael's view of the events of the incident. The defense reminded the jury that by Texas law Michael was not guilty of capital murder. The defense attorney told the jury that Michael feared for his life and the life of his family and was within the law to use deadly force when he did. He admitted that Michael did make some bad choices after the shooting, but he did go straight to the house and sit outside for about 10 minutes since the women had told him they had someone 10 minutes from the home if they called them. Everything looked okay, so he went to a construction area and put the gun under a pile of brush, then went and washed his car and went home. Michael testified that he was going to turn

150

himself in to the police the next morning after everyone left for church.

"That is this case in a nutshell, nothing more and nothing less. The District Attorney showed you blood evidence, DNA evidence, how and where the criminals were shot. They had their eyewitness come in and tell you she did not see anything and then give you lie after lie and a story about everything that happened, Why? Why the show? Why the drama? Why the fairy tale? The defendant never denied that he shot those two criminals, but the prosecution spent eight days spinning a tale and proving he pulled the trigger. They did not want you to see how they were protecting Cashman and his organization. You have seen direct testimony to some of the crimes they have committed, even other crimes in that county, but the only one charged was Michael for defending himself and his family. I ask you to come to the only conclusion that serves justice and find the defendant not guilty."

The District Attorney's Final Closing Argument

Now we have the "Golden Rule" I told you about. "I would like you to close your eyes and imagine 10 years from now and there is a young woman. She has been paroled from prison. She is in her early thirties. She admits to making a lot of bad mistakes in her life before prison, but while in prison she reformed and found God and has completely transformed her life. Now, she is out and working at a fast-food restaurant and continuing to better herself. Now imagine that is Cinnamon. That is what could have been the story, if the defendant had not acted as judge, jury, and executioner. Cinnamon was guilty of theft, that's all. It's a ten-year sentence in Texas. But the defendant gave her the death penalty."

The District Attorney stated that it was Michael's own fault, that if he had not contacted them he never would have met them. He told the jury that to believe Michael, "you must believe everything in his story, and the right and just thing is to convict the defendant of capital murder."

Chapter 40
Some Final Business

The judge stated there was some business to take care of. One of the jurors had tested positive for COVID and had symptoms. Another juror was scheduled to begin vacation that weekend. So, first he called in all the jurors first to see if anyone else had COVID symptoms. The jurors entered the courtroom, and they all denied experiencing any COVID symptoms. The juror that tested positive and had symptoms was excused.

Then, the juror that was scheduled to go on vacation in a few days was called up separately. The judge stated that if deliberations went on for a few days he could miss his trip and asked, "Are you okay with that?"

The juror looked puzzled and stated, "I will have to talk with my wife," so the judge allowed him a short break to call his wife.

The juror returned and stated, "I would hate to miss my trip, but I am really invested in this case and would like to see it through."

The judge asked, "So, are you staying or leaving? It's your choice."

The juror looked stunned and then answered, "I guess I am going."

Then the judge told him "Thank you for serving. You are excused."

Then the judge seated the two alternate jurors.

The judge stated, "It is about 11:00 a.m., so we are going to break for lunch and return at 1:00 p.m.; and at that time the jury will begin deliberations."

The judge told everyone to stay at the courthouse. Everyone thought that was odd, "He must be expecting a quick verdict. Does he know something we don't?"

During lunch, the District Attorney's office always brought the lunch to a large conference room for the families of Cinnamon and Jade. But there was something odd this time. Someone brought them a cake. The jury had not even started deliberating, and they were celebrating.

Chapter 41
The Verdict Is In

It was about 7:00 p.m., and Michael and his family were told to go into the courtroom. A lot of his supporters had already headed home and figured there would be no verdict today. His family thought that the judge would just dismiss court for the day at that time.

Then, Michael's dad saw the Assistant District Attorney look at Cinnamon's mother and say, "The verdict is in," and then almost immediately Cinnamon's mother looked at the court clerk and made a motion to her as if asking what the verdict was, and the court clerk nodded yes.

Everyone could hear the jury laughing loudly in the hallway leading to the jury room. Michael and his family and friends were all terrified and barely breathing, not making any sounds.

The judge walked into the courtroom holding a piece of paper and then called for the jury to come into the courtroom. The judge stated, "We have a verdict." Michael's family was shocked at such a quick verdict. The jury had only been deliberating for about 5 hours minus breaks, but okay, here we go. Michael turned and handed his father his cell phone and wallet, just in case. His dad had always told him to hope for the best but prepare for the worst.

The judge told Michael to rise, and he did as the judge ordered.

Now normally the judge asks the jury if they have reached a decision and then has the bailiff get that decision from the jury foreperson and give to the judge and then reads the verdict, but that was not the case here. It seemed like everyone knew what the verdict was except Michael and his family and friends and attorneys.

The Judge began to read: "On the charge of Capital Murder, the jury finds you GUILTY as charged, and you are sentenced to Life In Prison Without the Possibility of Parole. Please walk over to the bailiff." Michael began to cry, unable to believe what he just heard. Michael's mother had tears running down her cheeks, trying to stay strong for her son. His daughter was inconsolable as were many of Michael's friends and family in the courtroom.

Michael's father stood strong for his son, refusing to give those bastards the satisfaction of seeing his pain, but he was devastated and remains devastated to this day. But he remains determined to fight on until his son receives the justice he deserves. On that fall evening in November 2017, Michael did what he had to do to protect himself and his family. Now it's our turn to fight for Michael's freedom. We are determined to see Michael free again.

Michael was found guilty of Capital Murder of multiple persons and sentenced to life without parole in a Texas penitentiary. You will find an addendum in the back of this book with the actual Texas Penal Code for Capital Murder and justification for using deadly force. I told you in the beginning you would get the truth from beginning to the end. The names have been changed to protect the innocent and not to bring attention to the criminal's families. I know everyone reading this book is wondering what is missing.

"If those criminals were really committing those crimes, how did the jury find him guilty?" Michael's family asks that same question every day.

There is nothing in this story or the evidence that was left out except a chapter on injustice. Was this a rigged jury? We may never know. We do know that the prosecution made inappropriate comments outside of the jury room. We know that the District Attorneys lied and misled the jury. We also know the District Attorneys did not offer one shred of physical evidence to disprove Michael's claim of self-defense. The prosecution did not offer any expert rebuttal witnesses to contest the defense experts who agreed that Michael was justified in using deadly force that evening. Did the prosecution already know the verdict before the trial started and that's why all they did was spin lies and deception? Maybe someday we will know what really was going on in that rural courthouse. This is not the end of the story, it's just another beginning. Our faith will be the only thing that can get us through this unbearable nightmare. Until then, there is another innocent family man, a father, a son, a valued caregiver in the community, who is in prison, awaiting the long, long, long appeal process, and all the while we still hear those jurors laughing in the hallway.

Appendix

PENAL CODE

TITLE 5. OFFENSES AGAINST THE PERSON

CHAPTER 19. CRIMINAL HOMICIDE

Sec. 19.01. TYPES OF CRIMINAL HOMICIDE. (a) A person commits criminal homicide if he intentionally, knowingly, recklessly, or with criminal negligence causes the death of an individual.

(b) Criminal homicide is murder, capital murder, manslaughter, or criminally negligent homicide.

Acts 1973, 63rd Leg., p. 883, ch. 399, Sec. 1, eff. Jan. 1, 1974. Amended by Acts 1973, 63rd Leg., p. 1123, ch. 426, art. 2, Sec. 1, eff. Jan. 1, 1974; Acts 1993, 73rd Leg., ch. 900, Sec. 1.01, eff. Sept. 1, 1994.

Sec. 19.02. MURDER.
  (a) In this section:
    (1) "Adequate cause" means cause that would commonly produce a degree of anger, rage, resentment, or terror in a person of ordinary

temper, sufficient to render the mind incapable of cool reflection.

(2) "Sudden passion" means passion directly caused by and arising out of provocation by the individual killed or another acting with the person killed which passion arises at the time of the offense and is not solely the result of former provocation.

(b) A person commits an offense if he:

(1) intentionally or knowingly causes the death of an individual;

(2) intends to cause serious bodily injury and commits an act clearly dangerous to human life that causes the death of an individual; or

(3) commits or attempts to commit a felony, other than manslaughter, and in the course of and in furtherance of the commission or attempt, or in immediate flight from the commission or attempt, he commits or attempts to commit an act clearly dangerous to human life that causes the death of an individual.

(c) Except as provided by Subsection (d), an offense under this section is a felony of the first degree.

(d) At the punishment stage of a trial, the defendant may raise the issue as to whether he caused the death under the immediate influence of sudden passion arising from an adequate cause. If the defendant proves the issue in the affirmative by a preponderance of the evidence, the offense is a felony of the second degree.

Acts 1973, 63rd Leg., p. 883, ch. 399, Sec. 1, eff. Jan. 1, 1974. Amended by Acts 1973, 63rd Leg., p. 1123, ch. 426, art. 2, Sec. 1, eff. Jan. 1, 1974; Acts 1993, 73rd Leg., ch. 900, Sec. 1.01, eff. Sept. 1, 1994.

Sec. 19.03. CAPITAL MURDER.
 (a) A person commits an offense if the person commits murder as defined under Section 19.02(b)(1) and:
  (1) the person murders a peace officer or fireman who is acting in the lawful discharge of an official duty and who the person knows is a peace officer or fireman;
  (2) the person intentionally commits the murder in the course of committing or attempting to commit kidnapping, burglary, robbery, aggravated sexual assault, arson, obstruction or retaliation, or terroristic threat under Section 22.07(a)(1), (3), (4), (5), or (6);
  (3) the person commits the murder for remuneration or the promise of remuneration or employs another to commit the murder for remuneration or the promise of remuneration;
  (4) the person commits the murder while escaping or attempting to escape from a penal institution;
  (5) the person, while incarcerated in a penal institution, murders another:

(A) who is employed in the operation of the penal institution; or

(B)   with the intent to establish, maintain, or participate in a combination or in the profits of a combination;

(6) the person:

(A)   while incarcerated for an offense under this section or Section 19.02, murders another; or

(B)   while serving a sentence of life imprisonment or a term of 99 years for an offense under Section 20.04, 22.021, or 29.03, murders another;

(7) the person murders more than one person:

(A) during the same criminal transaction; or

(B)   during different criminal transactions but the murders are committed pursuant to the same scheme or course of conduct;

(8) the person murders an individual under 10 years of age;

(9) the person murders an individual 10 years of age or older but younger than 15 years of age; or

(10)   the person murders another person in retaliation for or on account of the service or status of the other person as a judge or justice of the supreme court, the court of criminal appeals, a court of appeals, a district court, a criminal district court, a constitutional county court, a statutory county court, a justice court, or a municipal court.

(b)   An offense under this section is a capital felony.

(c) If the jury or, when authorized by law, the judge does not find beyond a reasonable doubt that the defendant is guilty of an offense under this section, he may be convicted of murder or of any other lesser included offense.

Added by Acts 1973, 63rd Leg., p. 1123, ch. 426, art. 2, Sec. 1, eff. Jan. 1, 1974. Amended by Acts 1983, 68th Leg., p. 5317, ch. 977, Sec. 6, eff. Sept. 1, 1983; Acts 1985, 69th Leg., ch. 44, Sec. 1, eff. Sept. 1, 1985; Acts 1991, 72nd Leg., ch. 652, Sec. 13, eff. Sept. 1, 1991; Acts 1993, 73rd Leg., ch. 715, Sec. 1, eff. Sept. 1, 1993; Acts 1993, 73rd Leg., ch. 887, Sec. 1, eff. Sept. 1, 1993; Acts 1993, 73rd Leg., ch. 900, Sec. 1.01, eff. Sept. 1, 1994; Acts 2003, 78th Leg., ch. 388, Sec. 1, eff. Sept. 1, 2003.
Amended by:
Acts 2005, 79th Leg., Ch. 428 (S.B. 1791), Sec. 1, eff. September 1, 2005.
Acts 2011, 82nd Leg., R.S., Ch. 1209 (S.B. 377), Sec. 1, eff. September 1, 2011.
Acts 2019, 86th Leg., R.S., Ch. 1214 (S.B. 719), Sec. 2, eff. September 1, 2019.

Sec. 19.04. MANSLAUGHTER. (a) A person commits an offense if he recklessly causes the death of an individual.

(b) An offense under this section is a felony of the second degree.

Acts 1973, 63rd Leg., p. 883, ch. 399, Sec. 1, eff. Jan. 1, 1974. Renumbered from Penal Code Sec. 19.04 by Acts 1973, 63rd Leg., p. 1123, ch. 426, art. 2, Sec. 1, eff. Jan. 1, 1974. Amended by Acts 1987, 70th Leg., ch. 307, Sec. 1, eff. Sept. 1, 1987. Renumbered from Penal Code Sec. 19.05 and amended by Acts 1993, 73rd Leg., ch. 900, Sec. 1.01, eff. Sept. 1, 1994.

Self Defense

Sec. 9.31. SELF-DEFENSE. (a) Except as provided in Subsection (b), a person is justified in using force against another when and to the degree the actor reasonably believes the force is immediately necessary to protect the actor against the other's use or attempted use of unlawful force. The actor's belief that the force was immediately necessary as described by this subsection is presumed to be reasonable if the actor:

    (1) knew or had reason to believe that the person against whom the force was used:

(A) unlawfully and with force entered, or was attempting to enter unlawfully and with force, the actor's occupied habitation, vehicle, or place of business or employment;

(B) unlawfully and with force removed, or was attempting to remove unlawfully and with force, the actor from the actor's habitation, vehicle, or place of business or employment; or

(C) was committing or attempting to commit aggravated kidnapping, murder, sexual assault, aggravated sexual assault, robbery, or aggravated robbery;

    (2) did not provoke the person against whom the force was used; and

(3) was not otherwise engaged in criminal activity, other than a Class C misdemeanor that is a violation of a law or ordinance regulating traffic at the time the force was used.

(b)   The use of force against another is not justified:

(1) in response to verbal provocation alone;

(2) to resist an arrest or search that the actor knows is being made by a peace officer, or by a person acting in a peace officer's presence and at his direction, even though the arrest or search is unlawful, unless the resistance is justified under Subsection (c);

(3) if the actor consented to the exact force used or attempted by the other;

(4) if the actor provoked the other's use or attempted use of unlawful force, unless:

(A) the actor abandons the encounter, or clearly communicates to the other his intent to do so reasonably believing he cannot safely abandon the encounter; and

(B) the other nevertheless continues or attempts to use unlawful force against the actor; or

(5) if the actor sought an explanation from or discussion with the other person concerning the actor's differences with the other person while the actor was:

(A) carrying a weapon in violation of Section 46.02; or

(B)   possessing or transporting a weapon in violation of Section 46.05.

(c) The use of force to resist an arrest or search is justified:

(1) if, before the actor offers any resistance, the peace officer (or person acting at his direction) uses or attempts to use greater force than necessary to make the arrest or search; and

(2) when and to the degree the actor reasonably believes the force is immediately necessary to protect himself against the peace officer's (or other person's) use or attempted use of greater force than necessary.

(d) The use of deadly force is not justified under this subchapter except as provided in Sections 9.32, 9.33, and 9.34.

(e) A person who has a right to be present at the location where the force is used, who has not provoked the person against whom the force is used, and who is not engaged in criminal activity at the time the force is used is not required to retreat before using force as described by this section.

(f) For purposes of Subsection (a), in determining whether an actor described by Subsection (e) reasonably believed that the use of force was necessary, a finder of fact may not consider whether the actor failed to retreat.

Acts 1973, 63rd Leg., p. 883, ch. 399, Sec. 1, eff. Jan. 1, 1974. Amended by Acts 1993, 73rd Leg., ch. 900, Sec. 1.01, eff. Sept. 1, 1994; Acts 1995, 74th Leg., ch. 190, Sec. 1, eff. Sept. 1, 1995.

Amended by:

Acts 2007, 80th Leg., R.S., Ch. 1 (S.B. 378), Sec. 2, eff. September 1, 2007.

Sec. 9.32. DEADLY FORCE IN DEFENSE OF PERSON. (a) A person is justified in using deadly force against another:

> (1) if the actor would be justified in using force against the other under Section 9.31; and
>
> (2) when and to the degree the actor reasonably believes the deadly force is immediately necessary:

(A) to protect the actor against the other's use or attempted use of unlawful deadly force; or

(B) to prevent the other's imminent commission of aggravated kidnapping, murder, sexual assault, aggravated sexual assault, robbery, or aggravated robbery.

(b) The actor's belief under Subsection (a)(2) that the deadly force was immediately necessary as described by that subdivision is presumed to be reasonable if the actor:

> (1) knew or had reason to believe that the person against whom the deadly force was used:

(A) unlawfully and with force entered, or was attempting to enter unlawfully and with force, the actor's occupied habitation, vehicle, or place of business or employment;

(B) unlawfully and with force removed, or was attempting to remove unlawfully and with force, the actor from the actor's habitation, vehicle, or place of business or employment; or

(C) was committing or attempting to commit an offense described by Subsection (a)(2)(B);

(2) did not provoke the person against whom the force was used; and

(3) was not otherwise engaged in criminal activity, other than a Class C misdemeanor that is a violation of a law or ordinance regulating traffic at the time the force was used.

(c) A person who has a right to be present at the location where the deadly force is used, who has not provoked the person against whom the deadly force is used, and who is not engaged in criminal activity at the time the deadly force is used is not required to retreat before using deadly force as described by this section.

(d) For purposes of Subsection (a)(2), in determining whether an actor described by Subsection (c) reasonably believed that the use of deadly force was necessary, a finder of fact may not consider whether the actor failed to retreat.

Acts 1973, 63rd Leg., p. 883, ch. 399, Sec. 1, eff. Jan. 1, 1974. Amended by Acts 1983, 68th Leg., p. 5316, ch. 977, Sec. 5, eff. Sept. 1, 1983; Acts 1993, 73rd Leg., ch. 900, Sec. 1.01, eff. Sept. 1, 1994; Acts 1995, 74th Leg., ch. 235, Sec. 1, eff. Sept. 1, 1995.
Amended by:
Acts 2007, 80th Leg., R.S., Ch. 1 (S.B. 378), Sec. 3, eff. September 1, 2007.

Sec. 9.33. DEFENSE OF THIRD PERSON. A person is justified in using force or deadly force against another to protect a third person if:

(1)   under the circumstances as the actor reasonably believes them to be, the actor would be justified under Section 9.31 or 9.32 in using force or deadly force to protect himself against the unlawful force or unlawful deadly force he reasonably believes to be threatening the third person he seeks to protect; and

(2) the actor reasonably believes that his intervention is immediately necessary to protect the third person.

Acts 1973, 63rd Leg., p. 883, ch. 399, Sec. 1, eff. Jan. 1, 1974. Amended by Acts 1993, 73rd Leg., ch. 900, Sec. 1.01, eff. Sept. 1, 1994.

Sec. 9.34. PROTECTION OF LIFE OR HEALTH. (a) A person is justified in using force, but not deadly force, against another when and to the degree he reasonably believes the force is immediately necessary to prevent the other from committing suicide or inflicting serious bodily injury to himself.

(b) A person is justified in using both force and deadly force against another when and to the degree he reasonably believes the force or deadly force is immediately necessary to preserve the other's life in an emergency.

Acts 1973, 63rd Leg., p. 883, ch. 399, Sec. 1, eff. Jan. 1, 1974. Amended by Acts 1993, 73rd Leg., ch. 900, Sec. 1.01, eff. Sept. 1, 1994.

SUBCHAPTER D. PROTECTION OF PROPERTY

Sec. 9.41. PROTECTION OF ONE'S OWN PROPERTY. (a) A person in lawful possession of land or tangible, movable property is justified in using force against another when and to the degree the actor reasonably believes the force is immediately necessary to prevent or terminate the other's trespass on the land or unlawful interference with the property.

(b) A person unlawfully dispossessed of land or tangible, movable property by another is justified in using force against the other when and to the degree the actor reasonably believes the force is immediately necessary to reenter the land or recover the property if the actor uses the force immediately or in fresh pursuit after the dispossession and:

      (1) the actor reasonably believes the other had no claim of right when he dispossessed the actor; or

      (2) the other accomplished the dispossession by using force, threat, or fraud against the actor.

Acts 1973, 63rd Leg., p. 883, ch. 399, Sec. 1, eff. Jan. 1, 1974. Amended by Acts 1993, 73rd Leg., ch. 900, Sec. 1.01, eff. Sept. 1, 1994.

Sec. 9.42. DEADLY FORCE TO PROTECT PROPERTY. A person is justified in using deadly force against another to protect land or tangible, movable property:

      (1) if he would be justified in using force against the other under Section 9.41; and

(2) when and to the degree he reasonably believes the deadly force is immediately necessary:

(A) to prevent the other's imminent commission of arson, burglary, robbery, aggravated robbery, theft during the nighttime, or criminal mischief during the nighttime; or

(B) to prevent the other who is fleeing immediately after committing burglary, robbery, aggravated robbery, or theft during the nighttime from escaping with the property; and

(3) he reasonably believes that:

(A) the land or property cannot be protected or recovered by any other means; or

(B) the use of force other than deadly force to protect or recover the land or property would expose the actor or another to a substantial risk of death or serious bodily injury.

Acts 1973, 63rd Leg., p. 883, ch. 399, Sec. 1, eff. Jan. 1, 1974. Amended by Acts 1993, 73rd Leg., ch. 900, Sec. 1.01, eff. Sept. 1, 1994.

Sec. 9.43. PROTECTION OF THIRD PERSON'S PROPERTY. A person is justified in using force or deadly force against another to protect land or tangible, movable property of a third person if, under the circumstances as he reasonably believes them to be, the actor would be justified under Section 9.41 or 9.42 in using force or deadly force to protect his own land or property and:

(1) the actor reasonably believes the unlawful interference constitutes attempted or

consummated theft of or criminal mischief
to the tangible, movable property; or
(2) the actor reasonably believes that:
(A) the third person has requested his protection of the land or property;
(B) he has a legal duty to protect the third person's land or property; or
(C) the third person whose land or property he uses force or deadly force to protect is the actor's spouse, parent, or child, resides with the actor, or is under the actor's care.

Acts 1973, 63rd Leg., p. 883, ch. 399, Sec. 1, eff. Jan. 1, 1974. Amended by Acts 1993, 73rd Leg., ch. 900, Sec. 1.01, eff. Sept. 1, 1994.

Sec. 9.44. USE OF DEVICE TO PROTECT PROPERTY. The justification afforded by Sections 9.41 and 9.43 applies to the use of a device to protect land or tangible, movable property if:
(1) the device is not designed to cause, or known by the actor to create a substantial risk of causing, death or serious bodily injury; and
(2) use of the device is reasonable under all the circumstances as the actor reasonably believes them to be when he installs the device.

About the Author

I am a mother, a wife, self-employed, and now an author. My passion is raising my children and watching them grow into caring, responsible adults; and I am very proud of them. I am very proud of Michael.

The events in this book changed the reality that I had believed in regarding law and order and criminal justice and were the inspiration and motivation to write this book. And as there is more to this story, there will be more books in the future. This story does not, it can not end here.

Hopefully, this book will entertain my readers and give them new insights.